THE GHOST
IN YOUR
CHRISTMAS PRESENT

A NOVELLA
OF THE
ISSACHAR GATEKEEPER

L. G. Nixon

Fitting Words

The Ghost in Your Christmas Present

Copyright © 2021 by L. G. Nixon

Published by Fitting Words—www.fittingwords.net

Unless otherwise noted, Scripture quotations are taken from the Holy Bible, New International Version®, NIV®. Copyright © 1973, 1978, 1984, 2011 by Biblica, Inc.® Used by permission of Zondervan. All rights reserved worldwide. www.zondervan.com. The "NIV" and "New International Version" are trademarks registered in the United States Patent and Trademark Office by Biblica, Inc.®

Scripture quotations marked ASV are taken from the American Standard Version. Public domain.

Scripture quotations marked NLT are taken from the Holy Bible, New Living Translation, copyright © 1996, 2004, 2015 by Tyndale House Foundation. Used by permission of Tyndale House Publishers, Carol Stream, Illinois 60188. All rights reserved.

Scripture quotations marked NASB are taken from the (NASB®) New American Standard Bible®. Copyright © 1960, 1971, 1977, 1995 by The Lockman Foundation. Used by permission. All rights reserved. www.lockman.org.

Library of Congress Cataloging-in-Publication Data

Print ISBN: 978-1-7357748-7-9

Don't miss any of the adventures!

THE ISSACHAR GATEKEEPER

In memory of H. Lee Wietsma,
who always believed I could—so I did.

And from the children of Issachar came men and women of honor who were strong and valiant.

They had understanding to know what to do; to do justice, to love kindness, and to walk humbly with their High King.

—The Chronicles of Ascalon

Tell your cares to the High King. He will keep you and never let you be shaken.

—The Chronicles of Ascalon

Contents

A Knock on the Door

"I'm telling you, girlfriend, my mom sees ghosts!" Lucy plopped on the bed and stared at the cell phone with disbelief. Her best friend could be so obtuse sometimes. She pushed her cold feet under the coverlet. The heater in the SUV worked intermittently on good days and not so much today; hours after getting out of the car, she was still chilled to the bone.

"How can that be? She isn't a ghost hunter, doesn't believe in the spiritual realm, and yells like crazy when you mention it," said Schuyler, munching away and crinkling a wrapper. The sound carried through the microphone. "She's even threatened to put you in counseling."

Lucy rolled her eyes—Schuyler and food. "I haven't a clue how it happened, but it did. Mom flinched and nearly drove us into a ditch. My short life passed before my eyes!" said Lucy, throwing up her hands. "Then she babbled on about a big turquoise vehicle with no driver. So, I got out the Spectrescope, and what did I see? A huge blue car just as she said—only, I saw the driver! It was a female ghost."

Last summer, Lucy had purchased an old wooden trunk from a vendor at the flea market. Inside were oddities she called artifacts. Tarnished and made of a strange metal, the objects were magical. The Spectrescope, an overly large magnifying glass with an antique handle decorated with runes, was the most powerful artifact in the trunk. It not only allowed her to see and find ghosts and spirits but also held the Spirit Sword that helped her defeat daemons.

"What? We've only encountered one female ghost before. Are you sure?"

"Yes, I'm sure! What's up with all the questions? You're supposed to be helping me figure this out." Lucy threw herself back against the decorative pillows propped along the tufted headboard and crossed her arms, pinching the phone between her shoulder and ear.

"Wowza. Grumpy, are we?"

"That's another question!" Lucy scrunched her face as Schuyler snorted in her ear. "You're so helpful. You know that, right?"

"I'm trying to figure this out myself. I can't even get my head wrapped around all the implications." Schuyler paused and considered the facts they did know, carefully choosing her next words. "We know you are a ghost hunter and a gatekeeper for the Issachar Gate. You're to protect the gate and keep the Dark Prince, Darnathian, from finding the ancient magic. The gates are hidden portals leading to the heavenly city of Ascalon in the High King's realm, and there are twelve gates on earth. However, we're still trying to understand what all that means. And you come from a long line of gatekeepers. Right?"

"Yeah." Lucy sat up straighter and pulled the coverlet around her. Following Schuyler's train of thought was giving her chills.

"Could the lineage possibly come through your mom or grandma? Or maybe your granddad? It's a long shot, but what if it's true?"

"My mom? A gatekeeper? She's scared by a mouse! Can you really see her fighting and defeating a daemon?" Lucy was incredulous. "I follow what you're saying, but I think you are way off base here." Lucy went to the dresser where the Augur Sphere sat. A magical artifact, the Augur Sphere would sometimes give her a glimpse of a possible future. The timeline constantly fluctuated, depending on the decisions she chose to make. Its swirling smoke-filled globe was glowing softly, but it offered no images in the sphere.

"We weren't very courageous, either, when we first became ghost hunters. Sometimes it's overwhelming, but we are getting stronger the more we learn," said Schuyler.

"Yeah, I suppose. I mean, really? Is my mom from the lineage of Issachar? I don't think so." Lucy tapped a finger on the globe of the Augur Sphere. It responded with a happy burbling of changing colors. She pinched her lips and crawled back on the bed.

"It's still a possibility, Luce. She sees ghosts. How do you explain that?"

"Maybe the lineage is through my dad. I've never met him, and neither Dale nor I know anything about the guy. He just disappeared, and Mom never answers any questions." Lucy shivered and pulled the coverlet around herself.

"I suppose it could be, but doubtful. He left his family, after all, so he's probably not from a line of gatekeepers," said Schuyler. "I still think the lineage is on your mom's side. She did see a ghost car, so there must be a connection somewhere. She may know more about the spiritual realm than you think. It could explain why she gets so defensive when you mention it."

"Nah, I think the ghost influenced my mom somehow so she could see the apparition of the car but not the driver. It's the only explanation. I mean, I didn't see the car or the driver until I used the Spectrescope, and I'm the ghost hunter." Lucy rubbed her tired eyes.

"What about your grandma?" asked Schuyler, still pursuing her train of thought while chewing again. "You did say once before that your grandma could see ghosts. Remember?"

"Grandma used to tease me when I stayed for sleepovers. She told me about the little lady ghost in the black taffeta dress who haunted her house for a while. When you're little and hear an adult say something like that, it scares the daylights out of you. Did I believe her?" Lucy sighed deeply, her knuckles needling her forehead. "I don't know. Grandma Elliot does have an odd sense of humor."

"I guess that could explain a few things," snickered Schuyler. In response, a rude noise blurted through the phone. "Hey, I'm just saying!"

"Whatever."

"Have you told Mr. Bill or Ms. Vivian what happened? They may have some thoughts."

"No, I haven't said anything to them yet. What would I say? 'Hey, my mom, who doesn't believe in the spirit realm, is seeing ghosts. Isn't that funny? Ha ha.' " Lucy rolled her eyes. "Grandma wants us to live with her until things get settled, but I don't want to live in Grand Traverse Bay. I love the area, but this is home. Mom doesn't want to displace Dale in his last year of school either. Everything is mixed up. The fire really changed everything."

"I'm sure the McGoos will understand. They are your guardians. I would tell them if you get the chance."

"Yeah, you're right. I love Mr. Bill. He's always so cheerful. And Ms. Vivian bustles around, thinking of things we might need or enjoy. She's a wonderful cook, like your mom." Lucy stretched out under the coverlet, snuggled into the pillows, and yawned. "I'm exhausted just thinking about all this stuff, and we haven't had dinner yet. I hope there is chocolate for dessert. I need a caffeine buzz to finish my homework. Bleh."

"There are only a few more days before the holidays. I am ready for a break," said Schuyler. "I have some Christmas shopping to finish up. Want to go with Mom and me to the mall on Saturday? We'll pick you up on the way."

"Sure. I have to get a couple of gifts for Mom and Dale and a frame for the painting I did for Grandma. The McGoos gave me a new set of watercolor pencils and brushes. Mr. Bill said it was an early birthday gift since the fire destroyed my paints. He knows I like to doodle. It was his idea." She yawned again and stretched. "I think I'll paint them a landscape as their Christmas gift."

"Mr. Bill is too cute," said Schuyler. "Well, got to go, girlfriend. See you at school in the morning?"

"Yup. I better go help with dinner." Lucy giggled. "Wear your running shoes when we go to the mall. We're going to shop till we drop!"

＊　＊　＊

Jeannie Hornberger put the clean plates in the cupboard, pasted on a smile, and hugged Vivian goodnight. Then she trudged up the stairs to the guest room she called home. She quietly closed the door, sagged against its panels, and reached a hand to the dresser to steady herself. It had taken all she could do to keep from bursting into tears during dinner. The chatter around the dinner table between Lucy, Dale, and the McGoos did little to lift her mood.

She had updated her online work history and social accounts and reached out to staffing agencies, but she had yet to get a response. The insurance monies were dwindling into oblivion. Without the compassion and kindness of her dear neighbors, she didn't know where her family would be.

Seething with anger for their predicament, she still couldn't believe their two-hundred-year-old home had burned in an unexplainable fire that had raged through the old timber, reducing it to a pile of ashy rubble shortly after she lost her job. Now they lived with the McGoos, depending on them for shelter and even for meals. To say she was frightened for all their futures was an understatement.

The excuse she told her mother for not wanting to move—because Dale was in his senior year—was valid enough. Change can be precarious for a maturing teenage boy. It would be intolerable for him to start over in a new school in his last year without the company of friends. More importantly, she didn't want to live in Aunt Isabel's house in Grand Traverse Bay with her mother.

The stress was getting to her. Jeannie waggled her head back and forth, the memories digging deep wells in her soul. Her love for her mother was strong, but her desire for independence was stronger. After all, she was quite capable of taking care of herself and her family. But her mother's and auntie's belief in a spiritual realm had been the real reason for her rebellion. She sighed and opened a drawer.

Jeannie changed into her nightgown, turned off the lights, slipped beneath the bedcovers, and relaxed into the comforting gentleness of the foam mattress. If they ever had a real home again someday, she would get herself a luxurious bed like this one she thought as she drifted off to sleep.

Jeannie slumbered, the shadows deepened, and the night wore on.

Knock. Knock. Knock.

"Hmm, go away. I'm trying to sleep," murmured Jeannie, burrowing down into the covers and ignoring the summons.

Knock. Knock. Knock.

"Lucy, what do you want? I'm trying to sleep, and you're not helping!"

Knock. Knock. Knock.

Mumbling, Jeannie got up and pulled on her robe, then padded through the murky dark to the door and opened it. *What?* she wondered, glancing up and down the empty hallway. Shadows dimmed the corners near the ceiling where the feeble light from the night-light couldn't reach. The small, multihued stained-glass apparatus nestled in an electrical socket just above the carpet. She stared at it as though the object could tell her who was pranking her.

Convinced it was Lucy, Jeannie gathered the robe closer, marched down the hall to Lucy's room, opened the door, and peeked inside. Lucy was sleeping deeply in one of the matching twin beds, the covers askew, a leg hanging off the bed and her mouth open, snoring. Jeannie pulled in a breath, preparing to scold her daughter, then decided against it. Instead, she would have a harsh word with the girl in the morning. Turning, she padded back to her room.

After another glance up and down the empty hallway, she closed the door and crawled back in bed. Settling into the covers, she snugged them around her shoulders and prepared to go back to sleep.

Knock. Knock. Knock.

"Oh, for heaven's sake! Lucy, go back to bed. I'll deal with you in the morning, you prankster!" said Jeannie loudly. Staring at the ceiling in the ambient light from the window, she waited for her daughter to knock again. After several minutes, it was still quiet. Heaving a deep sigh, she closed her eyes and—

Knock. Knock. Knock.

"Lucy!" Jeannie yelled, exasperated. Grabbing the robe, she flung it around her shoulders and trudged to the door. Her hand reached for the doorknob, then paused and waited for the sound to come again.

Knock. Knock. Knock.

"Gotcha!" she said, whipping open the door. "What?" she gasped.

The hallway was empty.

Chills crept down her spine, and she felt the blood drain from her face. There was no way anyone could have moved that fast. She would have seen them. Was it possible she was dreaming? Or was this a reenactment of the haunting from her mother and dad's house when she was a teenager? Mother always maintained a ghost had haunted the house for a time. Tingles crept down her arms and legs, leaving a cold, uncomfortable sensation behind.

Jeannie turned and dove for the bed and pulled the covers over her head, leaving only a tiny open space for her nose so she could breathe. Even the robe she wore was not enough protection from the cold that slithered into her bones, chilling her.

The bedroom door slowly closed on its own.

Santa's Not So Jolly This Year

Lucy and Schuyler huddled at the back of the science lab and waited for the teacher to return with their test papers. The usually well-organized Mr. Bulman had left the tests in his briefcase, which was still in his car at the back of the slush-covered staff parking lot. Calculating the time, distance, and conditions, Lucy determined the class had ten minutes of free time at their disposal. While the rest of their classmates chattered and goofed around, Lucy and Schuyler discussed a Christmas surprise party they were planning for Lucy's mom. They hoped it would brighten her mom's mood. Grandma Elliot, who was coming for the holidays, was excited about the surprise party.

"Okay, let's see what we have so far. Are your mom and dad on board with this?" asked Lucy.

Schuyler rapidly nodded her head. "Oh yeah. Mom is bringing her chocolate triple-berry torte with buttercream frosting, and Dad will bring his blue cheese monster burgers to grill and some veggies. Does Mr. Bill have a large enough grill?" Schuyler had a dreamy look on her face, thinking about the torte her mom would be baking.

"Um, don't know. I'll ask Mr. Bill later. Mrs. McGoo is doing salads and, of course, a batch of her chocolate chip cookies," said Lucy, scribbling notes in her journal.

"You can never have too much chocolate, you know," said Schuyler, licking her lips.

"You and your food obsessions, girlfriend. It's a wonder you don't weigh a ton by now," said Lucy, ducking the hand Schuyler swiped at her. "Anyway, Mr. Bill will grill the veggies along with the burgers. It will be like a summer picnic in December."

"Ooh! I can't wait. Your mom is going to be so surprised. I only hope things start looking up for her. It's been a rough time all around," said Schuyler. Lucy's head slowly bobbed up and down.

"Okay, so we've got the foods taken care of," said Lucy, tapping the point of her pencil against the journal page. "What about board games? It's too cold and snowy to do anything outside unless we all go snowboarding."

"Didn't your snowboard burn up in the fire?"

"Drat, forgot about that. Guess it's going to be board games." Lucy pinched her lips into a thin line, her eyes rolling toward the ceiling. "I keep forgetting about all the things we used to have. Drat, drat, drat."

Just then, Mr. Bulman rushed into the science lab, dropped his briefcase, and slammed the door. He pushed against it as he peeked out the side transom window. His hair stood on end, and his clothes were disheveled. Murmurs rippled through the room.

"What happened to him?" whispered Schuyler. "He looks like he's seen a ghost." As soon as she said the word, Schuyler's eyebrows popped up, emphasizing the startled expression and the mouth that dropped open. "Oh no. You don't think—"

"Argh!" bellowed Mr. Bulman. The teacher turned, ducked behind his desk in the corner, and yelled, "Everyone get down! I don't know what that thing is!" Stools toppled and clattered to the floor as students squealed and ducked under the counters and hid behind the cabinets.

"It's a ghost!" someone yelled. There were gasps and more squeals. A few curious students peeked their heads out, their eyes nearly popping from their sockets as an apparition floated through the door and into the room.

The large, muscular apparition was opaque and translucent. He was dressed in a fur-trimmed red-velvet cloak and wearing a matching fur-trimmed hat with a pouf on the tip that hung over one shoulder. The ghost had a bright-pink, puffy face, a broad nose, and a long, dismal, shaggy gray beard and mustache. He sat astride a giant reindeer with antlers that cantered about the front of the room. Instead of carrying a bag of gifts, the ghost held a large wooden staff in one hand and the reins in the other.

Lucy grabbed the Spectrescope from her backpack and quickly stuffed it under her sweater, where it was easy to reach. Then, glancing nervously at Schuyler, who was staring at the ghost, Lucy fixed a grin on her face and stood.

"Hey! Great job, Mr. Bulman!" said Lucy, yelling over the frightened squeals of her classmates. "Where's the AV equipment? That's the best projection I've seen yet. It almost looks real!" She clapped her hands and whistled a catcall. Laughing, Lucy prodded Schuyler with her foot. Her friend slowly stood and clapped, then joined in the laughter with Lucy. Classmates got up from their hiding spots to stare at the ghost, realizing the specter must be a prank.

"Where'd you get such a scruffy-looking dude to play Santa?" said Lucy, motioning for the others to clap and laugh too. The din was getting louder. "The guy is *huge*, and everyone knows Santa is an *elf*. Scruffy, pudgy Santa would get stuck in the chimney!"

"Yeah! You're too huge to be Santa!" someone yelled.

"Oh, the poor reindeer!" another student shouted. Laughter rippled through the room, replacing the frightened squeals.

The reindeer stopped cantering, snorted, and pawed the floor. The Santa ghost glared in Lucy's direction. Angered by the scoffing, for daemons can't bear scorn, the spirit puffed up his chest and lifted his chin toward Lucy. Glaring, he raised the staff and pointed it ominously in her direction. The apparition turned the stag, and together they jumped through the classroom door and disappeared.

"Woo-hoo! Let's hear it for Mr. Bulman!" yelled Lucy as the others joined in. "Merry Christmas, Mr. Bulman!"

Schuyler grinned and poked an elbow into Lucy's ribs. Everyone was on their feet, clapping and stomping approval for the teacher's prank. Having entered the spirit of Halloween by decorating his classroom with a pipe-smoking skeleton wearing a tie, the Christmas prank seemed feasible.

Mr. Bulman shakily stood, straightened his clothes, and smiled uncertainly at the class. He motioned to the class to take their seats and waited for them to settle down before retrieving the test papers from the briefcase. Walking among the students, he slowly returned their tests. When he reached Lucy and Schuyler, he paused, scribbled something on the top sheet, and handed it to Lucy before walking on.

Lucy pinched her lips together as her face scrunched into a scowl, and she showed the sheet to Schuyler. She watched as her friend's lips puckered into a circle. The note read, "I'll see you after class, Miss Hornberger."

"What did Mr. Bulman want to talk about after class?" asked Schuyler as she closed her locker door and leaned against it. Students milled around, some drifting to their after-school activities, others rushing to catch the bus. "Please tell me Mr. Bulman didn't blame you for the apparition. He didn't give you detention, did he?" Concern clouded her hazel-green eyes. "You don't need another detention."

"No, but he certainly thinks I had something to do with it." Lucy threw her hands up. "Every time his classroom is disturbed, he thinks I had something to do with it. You know, this gets irritating after a while," she grumbled, spinning the combination lock on her door. "Last week someone hung a stuffed toy turkey from the ceiling in front of his door. Each time the door whacked it, it gobbled. So, naturally, because of my effervescent personality, he thought I did it." Schuyler snickered. Lucy squinted at her.

"Sorry, girlfriend. But it does sound like something you would do," said Schuyler, dipping her head to hide a smirk, her long blonde curls partially obscuring her face.

"Ha ha, you're so funny, honey," groused Lucy. Then a smirk dimpled her cheeks, and she snorted. "I did think about pranking him, but with everything else going on, I thought better of it. Mom has more trouble than she can handle right now. She doesn't need me adding to it."

"What are we going to do about the ghost? Should we go after him tonight? He looked a particularly nasty sort, the way he pointed his staff at you." Schuyler hefted her book bag onto her shoulder. "It was brilliant, by the way. You sneered him right out of the room. You did that to the first ghost we had to vanquish."

"Well, we know daemons are excessively proud and don't like to be mocked. At least it bought us a little time," Lucy said. "I wonder if Scruffy Santa is behind some of the odd happenings around the school. I overheard Mr. Bill telling Vivian about some unusual activity, like unlocked doors and misplaced things." The locker door squeaked as she pushed it open, leaned in, retrieved her sneakers from the bottom, and stuffed them in the backpack.

"Wouldn't Mr. Bill have mentioned it to you? He knows you're a ghost hunter."

"Eh, maybe it didn't seem like it was important enough to mention." She shoved her textbooks on the shelf. "It could be teenagers messing around too. I can ask him when I get home." She grabbed her coat from the hook, slipped it on, and closed the door. An odd look flittered across her features. "Wow," she whispered.

"What?" asked Schuyler, zipping her jacket.

"The McGoos' house is home. It's altogether comforting and weird at the same time." A frown puckered her brows. "How strange is that, girlfriend?"

"I think it's great. Even I think of the McGoos as part of my family. They're pretty special, you know?" Schuyler's face scrunched suddenly, followed by a convulsive shiver. "Wowza! I'm cold!" She glanced about but didn't see the ghost.

Lucy grabbed the Spectrescope from its pocket in the backpack and scanned the corridor. Standing a few feet behind Schuyler was the scruffy ghost in the Santa cloak. The scowl on his face indicated he wasn't in a jolly mood. He casually slapped the rod against his open palm.

"Schuyler, get behind me. The Santa ghost is just over there, and he's glaring at us." Lucy pointed toward the junction of the corridors. "Follow my lead, okay? I want him to follow us to the science lab. There shouldn't be anyone down there at this time of day."

"I'll be right behind you!" said Schuyler, checking her wrist for her magical bracelet. It could transmute into a shield, and it also contained her broad sword sheathed on the back of the shield. In addition, she wore a plaid vest and a beret, which were magical. These became her breastplate and helmet. Lucy had armor too.

"Catch me if you can, Scruffy!" yelled Lucy, darting toward the main staircase housed in the turret of the century-old school building that was reminiscent of a castle. Schuyler dashed alongside as they hurried down the circular steps to the lower level. The lights down the corridor were in power-saving mode; every other fixture was on, casting weird shadows along its length.

Dashing into the empty science lab, they found the under-cabinet lights were off, but the fluorescent overheads were still lit. Study notes were scrawled across the chalkboard in Mr. Bulman's scratchy handwriting.

Lucy turned and raised the Spectrescope, expecting to see the velvet-clad ghost in the lens. But instead, her eyes widened as the spirit came striding confidently into the room, fully visible, very large, and very angry. He still carried the club-like wooden staff.

"Spirit Sword!" said Lucy. The bracelet morphed into her shield, and her armor appeared. Her spare sword, Rathanael, was sheathed near the handgrip. The Spectrescope head retreated into the handle, followed by a molten blue metal that emerged and became the sword. It glowed with an ethereal blue light. Schuyler's armor had transformed too.

The ghost gathered his velvet cloak around him and stared at the armor clad teenage girls pointing weapons at him. He threw his head back and laughed. The sound was soft and musical and unexpected from such a fierce-looking face. The pink cheeks had gone to red, and his eyes narrowed. He wasn't a jolly old elf bearing gifts. He was an entity to be feared.

"In the name of the High King, tell me your name!" said Lucy, brandishing the Spirit Sword. Slight tremors rippled through her body, conflicting with the confidence projected in her voice. Every ghost vanquishing was different, and although Lucy needed to be courageous, it was easier said than done. She swallowed hard.

"Such a brave little thing you are," said the ghost. A smile creased the rosy cheeks, but it didn't reach the eyes. "My name, dear lady, is Furfurcas. I am a knight in the Under Realm of the Dark Prince. My liege, Darnathian, has given me command of twenty leagues of Daemonimini. And you come against me with your little sword? Now, how cute is that!" sneered Furfurcas, his voice soft and gentile. He leaned on the staff and laughed, the sound booming through the room, while his eyes glittered like black diamonds, cold and soulless in a sea of red.

Furfurcas Has a Fur Pouf

3

Lucy widened her stance, her feet firmly planted, and raised her sword at the angry spirit wrapped in a red-velvet cloak and hat. He was much larger than she had expected. When they'd seen him earlier, it was as though the ghost was projecting through the astral plane and wasn't really in the classroom. Although the threatening gestures he had made were real enough.

She stole a glance at Schuyler, whose eyes were stuck in wide-open mode and staring at the huge specter. The sword, Zazriel, glimmered with the same ethereal blue light as Lucy's Spirit Sword. The blades were indestructible and razor sharp. Each was adorned with jewels and an unknown language. Lucy was glad they had them.

"What do you want, Furfurcas? If that's your real name," Lucy scoffed. "You know, it reminds me of those foo-foo lattes Schuyler gets at the coffee shop. All whipped cream and no substance."

Schuyler leaned sideways, her head tilted next to Lucy's, and whispered, "Is that wise to provoke this dude?" She kept Zazriel pointed at the Santa daemon. "Kind of like poking the bear, isn't it?" Her blonde curls vibrated from nervousness. Lucy bit back a remark, only because she was experiencing the same quaking.

Lucy raised the sword. "In the name of the High—"

Furfurcas whipped his hand and pushed a great blast of sulfur-laden air at them. The force pitched them backward, hurtling them through the air with their arms and legs outstretched. The girls smacked the wall, rattling the blinds on the windows above them. Their metal armor clattered, their shields and swords clanging loudly in the empty room as they slid to the floor. Furfurcas laughed and leaned his staff against the chalkboard rail. He placed his hands on his ample hips and studied the girls' reaction. He whipped a hand to the side and pushed the air. The workstations in front of him ripped from their footings, slid across the floor, and smacked into the stations behind, enlarging the space.

"Whoa!" said Lucy, scrambling to her feet, coughing and gagging. She grabbed Schuyler's hand and pulled her up. "Okay, nice one, Furball," Lucy said, her eyes watering from the sulfur. She rapidly blinked, sending tears dribbling down her cheeks. Schuyler had red blotches on her face where the gases had burned the skin. She was dry heaving from the stench.

Furfurcas raised his hand again. Lucy, anticipating another hit, raised her shield. With one foot forward, she blocked the sulfuric blast, and it dissipated. Schuyler, pulling in a quick breath, raised her shield and caught the third blast the daemon ghost sent at them. The spirit, irritated at their survival, moved his arms like windmills, his cupped hands directing the gases at them. The girls repeatedly blocked the invisible missiles, safe behind their shields.

Lucy saw a container on the counter at the back of the room heaped with large cotton balls used for science experiments. She grabbed it and, cupping her hand, whipped her arm forward toward the ghost. The cotton balls shot from the container, zoomed through the air, and pelted the unsuspecting entity. While it couldn't possibly harm him, the assault did irritate him.

His anger increasing, he opened his mouth wide and yelled. Several well-aimed cotton balls lodged in his mouth, stuffing his cheeks and muffling his voice. Schuyler squealed with laughter. Stomping and spitting the cotton out, he glared at them and increased his efforts, whipping his arms and sending blasts of sulfur at them. The air in the room was nearly unbreathable. Lucy gagged, and her eyes were streaming.

"Shimmer Shield!" she yelled. The anomaly surrounded them. It was an invisible bubble of protection she was able to call forth using the power of the Spectrescope. The air inside the shield was sweet and refreshing. The sulfur bombs could not penetrate the Shimmer Shield; however, she couldn't fight back either. At least it gave the girls a brief respite from the onslaught.

Remembering a previous encounter with a daemon where Lucy was able to project an energy blast from the Spirit Sword, she dropped her shield just as the daemon directed another blow at them. "Shield down!" she yelled. Fire erupted from the tip of her blade, igniting the gases in a brief but thunderous explosion. The fireball quickly dispersed, leaving only the stench of burned gases behind.

"Good one, Luce!" said Schuyler, holding her sword and shield in front of her.

The ghost was angry now. He swung both arms, hands cupped, and, stepping into the motion, shoved the invisible missile toward them. Trusting the Spectrescope's power, Lucy stepped into the missile with the sword. The sword tip emitted a jet of flame, igniting the gases, and pushed flames back at the ghost. The flare-up was brief but rather satisfying. She smirked at Schuyler, who did a fist pump.

Furfurcas leaned back and threw up an arm to protect his eyes, but his beard and mustache were singed and smoldering. The fur of his cloak and hat wafted little smoky tendrils, which drifted slowly upward. He slapped his beefy hands against his beard and mustache to disperse the flames.

"A lucky move, human. You are quick to react, but you don't take the initiative to act *first*. Why is that, I wonder? Could it be you are insecure in your abilities?" asked Furfurcas, his voice returning to the soft genteel resonance as before. He leaned against the counter, waved away the wispy smoke, and then clasped his hands benignly in front of him. "It is a reasonable assumption; you are human and fighting against eternal forces. How could you possibly expect to win? I would leave and let the eternal beings alone. You are finite and dispensable and poorly trained. If your High King loves you, why didn't he fully equip you for such a momentous task?" said the daemon benevolently and looking more like a kindly grandfather in a crispy Santa cloak. "My dear girls, it isn't even your battle."

"Yeah, I've wondered that too. Why didn't the High King give us better training before dropping us into this ongoing fight?" asked Schuyler, confusion puckering her brow as she stared at Lucy.

"Don't listen to him, Schuyler. He is trying to distract us," said Lucy, glancing at her companion. "Everything he is saying is untrue."

"Is it?" asked Schuyler, distracted. Her confidence was wavering.

Suddenly, solid yet unseen bands wrapped around each of them as Furfurcas whipped his arms toward the girls, his hands making circular motions. The invisible cords were squeezing them tighter and tighter. It was becoming difficult to breathe.

"Lucy, do something," gasped Schuyler as she struggled against the mysterious bonds crushing the life out of her. Holding her last breath, she tried to keep her ribs from collapsing.

"I'm trying!" Lucy slammed herself against the wall and struggled to free the hand holding the sword. She got the Spirit Sword into position. "Blast that daemon!" she yelled and pointed the blade at the ghost.

A stream of ethereal blue energy discharged in a series of shock waves, encompassing the daemon and blasting him against the wall like a rag-doll Santa. The bonds dissolved. Their arms and legs were free.

The daemon crumpled to the floor, stunned. After a moment, he snatched his staff from the floor. With surprising speed, he gained his feet and charged them.

"You are mincemeat, stupid humans!" he yelled. He raised the staff over his head and swung the club. "Prepare to meet your doom from the knight of the Under Realm!"

Lucy stood with one foot ahead of the other, sword ready. The daemon swung. Lucy stepped aside, and Furfurcas stumbled past, his staff meeting no resistance. He quickly turned. Lucy struck with the Spirit Sword, the force nearly knocking the rod from the daemon's hand as he tried to block her attack.

Gripping the rod two-fisted, he parried each move Lucy could make. She blocked each of his strikes. He swung again. This time she used a counter cut and brought the sword down. It circled and deflected his weapon.

Growling, the daemon Santa raised his arms, his staff over his head, and angrily started his downward swing. Lucy jumped and thrust her foot into the ghost's belly. He doubled over, dropped the staff, and staggered backward. The pouf on the tip of his hat dangled in his face as he gasped for breath.

Schuyler moved in and took a position next to Lucy with her sword at the ready. Now both girls advanced toward the ghost, alternately swinging and deflecting the blows from the thick wooden staff. The ghost couldn't gain on the two girls; he stepped back with each strike.

Finally, the daemon was pinned against the wall like an insect. He cursed and screamed, his voice booming through the room.

Schuyler grimaced, hoping the ghost's yelling didn't carry beyond the lower level of the old school building. The last thing they needed were curious innocents getting in harm's way.

Lucy stepped closer to the daemon and lifted his chin with the point of the Spirit Sword. Furfurcas lowered his voice, then growled at her.

"So, the rumors are true. You are powerful, for a human girl," said the ghost. His eyes glittered dangerously. "You may be courageous, but you will regret tangling with me. One of these days, when you see me, you won't fare so well."

"I think you're mistaken. You are the one cowering at the end of my sword," said Lucy. The sword quivered slightly in her hand. She never liked being this close to a dangerous entity. She held her chin higher and stared back at the daemon. "Now, in the name of the—"

The ghost grinned and imploded with a pop.

"Where did he go?" Lucy yelled, frantically looking around the room. The room was empty, and the daemon ghost was gone.

"What do you mean? You just defeated him!" asked Schuyler, incredulous. Her grip on the shield and sword went limp, lowering the weapons.

"No! I didn't. He simply vanished before I could learn his real daemon name," said Lucy. Her shoulders drooped, and she blew out a long breath, puffing her cheeks.

"Do you think he's gone, or could he be around here somewhere?" asked Schuyler, waving a hand in front of her face. The stench of burned gases was still rather pungent. "Ew!" She stuck her tongue out, gagging.

"Well, wherever he went, he left a mess behind," said Lucy. Tapping into the power of the Spirit Sword, she raised her hand toward the displaced workstations. "RESTORE!" Like an old movie projector running backward, the scene reversed itself. The workstations slid back into place, the blinds straightened their crooked slats, and the container refilled with the cotton balls. The disheveled room was nearly back to the way Mr. Bulman had left it, but it still smelled like rotten eggs. Schuyler grimaced and waved a hand under her nose.

"Hey!" said Lucy. "Our armor morphed. We're back in our regular clothes. It must mean—"

"LUCY HORNBERGER! What is the meaning of this?" bellowed Mr. Bulman, standing in the doorway and waving a hand under his nose. "*Now* what did you do?"

". . . I'm in trouble. Again," whimpered Lucy.

More Trouble

4

"Lucy Hornberger! What is wrong with you? Another detention? Igniting harmful gases in the science lab unsupervised? Singeing the ceiling?" Jeannie Hornberger stared openmouthed at her daughter as though the teenager belonged to someone else. "I can't pay the car insurance, let alone replace the ceiling tiles in the science lab!"

Lucy's head drooped so far she looked as though she might topple over. "I have another week of detention to do after the holidays too," she whispered.

"Aw, Jeannie, don't be so hard on the girl," Mr. Bill chimed in. "They were only doing a science experiment—in the science lab, no less. I'm sure the school has plenty of replacement tiles lying about somewhere. I'll look for them

The Ghost Writer

when I get to school in the morning." As a custodian, he was responsible for repairs anyway. He put a hand on Lucy's shoulder and gave a comforting squeeze. Jeannie threw up her hands, spun on her heel, and stomped up the stairs.

"It's okay, Mr. Bill," said Lucy, glancing at the older gentleman. "I'm getting used to being in trouble all the time. I have babysitting monies I can donate to the fund, so mom doesn't have to pay all of the damages."

"You're a good girl, Lucy. I'm sure your mom will appreciate the gesture once she calms down a bit. You did kind of spring it on her, you know." His brown hair was tousled again, reminding Lucy of a cairn terrier dog with a bad hair day.

"Yeah, I've learned it's best just to get it over. I'm going to get yelled at anyway." She wandered to the kitchen where Vivian was finishing dinner preparations.

"There are some chocolate chip cookies in the pantry, dearie. Maybe something sweet will help the bitters go down a little easier. What do you think? Have a cookie?" asked Vivian, her spoon held midair.

"I'd better pass on the cookies till after dinner. It would be another infraction if Mom sees me eating sweets before protein." Lucy sat on the counter stool and rested her head in her hands, elbows on the counter. "Can I help you with anything, Ms. Vivian?"

Vivian reached over the island counter and patted Lucy's cheek. "How about setting the dinette table for me? Dinner is almost ready. By the time you complete your task, dinner will be done." She stirred a tapioca pudding simmering on the stove top with her big wooden spoon.

"Thanks for everything you do for us, Ms. Vivian," said Lucy, taking the place mats from the drawer. "I don't know what we would do without you and Mr. Bill. There's no way we can ever repay you." She placed the cutlery and plates next.

"Sweetheart, there's no need to repay anything. You're family, in more ways than one. It's a blessing to Bill and me to be able to help. And you know how much we love you." Vivian smiled at Lucy, then turned back to the stove top. She poured the pudding into a serving bowl and set it on the sideboard to cool. "Oh dear, the bowl is too small. There is a little pudding left in the pan. Want to *clean* it for me?" she said with a wink.

Lucy snorted. "I'd be happy to *clean* and wash the pan for you, Ms. Vivian." Scrapping the pot, she spooned a heaping portion of warm pudding into her mouth and licked the remnants from the spoon. Her cheeks creased in a smile as she savored the sweet concoction. The bumpy texture was unique, fun, and delicious.

"Oh, Ms. Vivian. I don't know who can cook better— you or Mrs. Williams. You're both such talented ladies. Wow, this is good!" Scrapping as much pudding from the pan as she could, she finally placed it in the soapy water and scrubbed it clean.

"Becca Williams is an exceptional cook and baker. I must admit, her cakes and tortes are beyond my doing. I'm good but not that good. Although my cookies are better." She scrunched her nose and giggled. "I love that dear lady too."

"Lucy Hornberger! Get up here! I want to talk to you, young lady!" Mom yelled down the stairway.

Lucy pinched her lips together, dipped her head, and dried her hands on the towel. "Ding, ding, ding. Round two!" she muttered as she trudged up the stairs. Vivian paused, glanced toward the ceiling, then took the roast from the oven.

"Did you set off a stink bomb in here? Wait till Ms. Vivian finds out what you did! The stench is horrible. What has gotten into you?" Her mom's scrunched face looked like she had eaten a sour pickle.

"What? No!" said Lucy. "I would never do that to the McGoos. And I haven't even been upstairs yet. I was in the kitchen helping Ms. Vivian." She waved a hand to disperse the odor, her face puckering as she went to the window and opened it.

"It must have been you," said her mom. "Is that what you were doing after school hours in the science lab? Making stink bombs?" Disappearing into the hall, she returned shortly with a towel from the bathroom and fanned the odor out the window.

"I'm telling you: *I didn't do it!*" Lucy stomped her feet.

"It had to be you! Who else would do such a nasty thing? Your brother?" Jeannie frantically waved the towel.

"What's all the yelling? Whoa!" said Dale, gagging from the odor. "Is there a problem with the bathroom plumbing? That's horrible!" He stood in the open doorway, waving a hand. "Gross! I can taste it in my mouth."

"Lucy's in trouble again at school, and now she's letting off stink bombs," groused Mom.

"I did not!" Lucy squinted at Dale when she saw him turn away, smirking. His footsteps faded as he went down the stairs.

"Whatever! You are grounded until you're twenty-three! I don't even know what to tell Vivian. I guess she'll figure it out since the whole house is going to stink. C'mon, let's go have dinner." Lucy followed her mom down the stairs, glaring at her back and not knowing what to think.

Jeannie hadn't eaten much at dinner; she'd mostly just moved the food around on her plate. Now, she sat on the bed reviewing the disappointment of the day. One hand curled into the neckline of her robe, and the other rubbed her forehead, trying to massage away the ache. The companies she had contacted had no interest in hiring, saying only that her skill set was either insufficient or overqualified for any available openings.

44   The Ghost Writer

Really?

Her mind was a jumble of angry thoughts over her unemployment and the untenable hope of holding her family together. Their future was hanging in the balance. She could only hope that selling the antiques she'd inherited from her aunt and the few monies in the trust fund would be enough to put them all back on stable footing. How sad that she had to rely on the benevolence of others.

Jeannie placed the robe over the foot of the bed and slipped beneath the covers. *What on earth is Lucy thinking? Why is she causing more problems at school?* she thought wearily. *I hope I can sleep tonight without any of her dumb shenanigans.* She pulled the covers close and drifted off to sleep.

Her dreams were filled with strange imagery. People surrounded her, glowing like fireflies and whispering. It made her feel uneasy; she tossed and turned. A few times, she woke thinking she'd heard someone calling her name. She tried to remember the resonant, deep, and comforting voice. It evoked feelings of something she had lost and desperately needed to find. But she was alone in a strange bedroom; though well appointed to comfort, it was not her room. She was a guest, dependent on others and loathing every moment of it. Finally, anger drove the dream away, and she turned over, punched the pillow, and tried to go back to sleep.

Knock. Knock. Knock.

"Oh, not again! What is that girl thinking?" said Jeannie as she got up, grabbed the robe, and stomped to the door. She paused, waiting.

Knock. Knock. Knock

"Lucy Hornberger, so help me!" Jeannie shouted, whipping open the door and stepping forward to confront the perpetrator, but she gasped instead. The hallway was as empty as it had been the night before. Her hand flew to her chest, and she closed her eyes. *No, no, no. It's stress, that's all it is*, she thought. *Stress will do strange things to a person.* Rolling her eyes to the ceiling, she sighed deeply.

Her limbs began to tremble as a brilliant column of light gradually appeared at the end of the hallway, hovering above the stairs. Jeannie stared at the apparition, then she slammed the door and shoved a chair under the doorknob. *Cold, I'm so cold*, she thought, grabbing the robe and snuggling into it. Jeannie crawled into bed and pulled the covers up, shivering with the cold or with fright; she wasn't sure which. *Stress, it's just stress.*

Jeannie closed her eyes and breathed deeply, aware of her breath and the respirations. She was beginning to relax when she became mindful of a presence in the room. Keeping her eyes closed, she was determined to ignore the sensation. All the stress, and lack of sleep, was playing havoc with her mind.

"Jeannie," said a voice as soft as rain.

Her eyes flew open. A bolt of fear shot through her. The column of light from the hallway hovered near the end of her bed. Fear kept her pinned to the bed, unable to move. A figure stood there, bathed in light—or was she made of light? Jeannie wanted to run, but her limbs wouldn't respond. Instead, a painful tingling coursed through her unwilling body.

"Jeannie," said the entity. "Do not be afraid. I mean you no harm. I have come to help you find your way home."

"Who . . . who are you?" said Jeannie, still quaking beneath the covers. The bedcovers vibrated with her quaking. The entity, bathed in light, was lovely. She had long golden hair pulled back from her face, the curls cascading about her head and shoulders. The pale-blue chiffon dress had narrow sleeves cuffed in lace, and there was a tuft of lace at the neck and laid in folds to frame her long hair and rosy-hued skin.

"My name is Helena, and I have come to help you remember."

"No! I don't believe in spirits. Go away!" said Jeannie, pulling the covers over her head and pushing further down into the safe confines of the dark and away from the entity. "Go away! You are not real. You're not real." She whimpered under the covers.

"Do not resist, Jeannie. You must wake up and remember," Helena said softly. She floated closer to the bed and leaned over the lump under the covers. "Wake up, Jeannie. And remember."

"No! I don't know what you mean!" said Jeannie, her voice muffled. When, after several minutes, there was still no answer, she slowly pushed the blankets back.

The room was empty.

Carols and Perils at the Mall

"Okay, so where to now?" asked Lucy, rummaging through the backpack for her list. "I have one more item to get; the frame for Grandma's painting." Pushing things around inside the bag, she found her list and checked off the item she'd just purchased. Schuyler was staring down the opposite aisle.

The grade-school carolers onstage in the center of the mall finished their concert and streamed from the platform, joining the proud parents who were gathered around the North Pole Village and Workshop and clapping loudly. A notice on a signpost said Santa was feeding his reindeer and would return shortly.

Christmas lights twinkled and blinked up and down the aisles, their strands hidden in the artificial evergreen boughs.

Christmas trees and wreaths adorned nearly every surface and storefront in the mall. Holiday music blared from the speakers, combining with the crowds to increase the noise level. Kids squirmed and squealed, running from tired parents while others romped in the play area with oversized replicas of food.

Schuyler stared at the giant hamburger with a little boy sitting on it. She looked at her watch, then down the aisle toward the food court. "You know, we could get some lunch. The lines aren't too busy right now. What do you want to eat?"

"Did I say I was hungry? We can keep shopping, then go for pizza later," said Lucy, smirking.

"Aw! I'm hungry now."

"It's not even noon!" said Lucy. "How can you be hungry? Didn't you have breakfast?" When Schuyler pouted, Lucy grinned. "I'm joking! We can get burgers." She poked an elbow into her friend's ribs. "I want a Buffalo Bill burger with the works and a chocolate shake. I'm so hungry, I could eat two." The backpack vibrated on her shoulder. "Uh-oh," she said, slipping it off and unzipping the bag.

"What's going on? Did you get a phone message?" asked Schuyler, still looking toward the food court and trying to decide what to eat.

"I don't think it was the phone. It was the Spectrescope. Look!" said Lucy, pulling the bag open to see the Spectrescope nestled inside. The rune symbols glowed on the ring around the base of the scope, moving like molten metal, changing shape, and forming new characters. The figures were disturbing—especially the Santa-shaped symbol.

"Oh no! Luce, you don't think Furfurcas followed us here, do you? I was hoping he would be confined to the school." Schuyler looked anxiously at Lucy, hoping her friend could come up with a different explanation.

"We defeated all the ghosts at school, so where did this one come from?" Lucy's eyebrows drew together as she twirled her bracelet. "Mom blamed me the other night for setting off a stink bomb in her room. I didn't consider it at the time, but maybe it was the ghost; maybe he followed me home." Careful to move only her eyes and not tip off the ghost, she searched for any indication Furfurcas was nearby.

"Oh, that's scary. Home is supposed to be safe," said Schuyler. Her eyes widened. "Wait—didn't the McGoos know he was in the house?" A hand flew to her open mouth as Lucy shrugged. "How could they not know?"

"Or maybe the McGoos knew and said nothing because Mom and Dale don't believe in the spiritual realm." Lucy stared at the Spectrescope, hoping it would give her an indication if something were about to happen. So far, so good. She slipped the backpack on and settled the bag firmly on her back.

"Good point. How would you explain everything that has happened? It's going to sound like nonsense to someone who doesn't believe."

"Uh-oh. The Spectrescope vibrated; the symbols are glowing again." Lucy's eyebrows shot upward. "Is that a *wind* emoji?"

Schuyler peeked at the lens and nodded. "It sure looks like it. But I wonder what—never mind," said Schuyler, grimacing and waving a hand in front of her face. "I think we know *that* fragrance." People were starting to notice the stench and murmuring.

"It's coming from the food court," said Lucy, stashing the scope inside her jacket and heading down the aisle toward the Buffalo Bill's Burger stand. They hurried unnoticed past a security guard, then Lucy did an abrupt turn and ran back.

The gray-haired security guard smiled as she rushed up to him. "Can I help you?" he asked.

"Sir! I think there's a major gas leak in the food court area." She reached a hand toward him, her face fearful and eyes pleading. "Isn't there something in the gas to make it stink like rotten eggs? The smell over there is awful," she said, pointing down the aisle toward Buffalo Bill's. "You should evacuate the area before someone gets hurt!"

The security guard frowned, noticing the odor. He clicked a handset attached at his shoulder as he hurried toward the food court, Lucy and Schuyler following behind.

"Central, we have a report of a gas leak in the food court. Better get someone down here to help clear the area while I check it out." His radio chirped as the dispatcher responded. "Confirmed. I detect a strong odor, like rotten eggs," the guard replied.

"Great idea, Luce!" whispered Schuyler, jogging beside Lucy.

Their sneakered feet were nearly soundless as they followed the guard. Lucy grabbed Schuyler's elbow and propelled her toward the abandoned Misty Orange soda stand. They slid undetected through the unlatched accordion security fence and hid behind the curtain to the back room.

It was dark and musty, and hopefully no one would look for them in the supply room. Moreover, the pop stand had been closed for months. Lucy removed the Spectrescope from her jacket, uttering a silent plea for the Shimmer Shield. It would prevent the security people from finding them.

They could still hear the security guard speaking, though they didn't hear much of the other responses. Lucy watched him through the slit in the curtain.

"Confirmed!" said the guard, clicking his handset. "Clearing the area now. Roger, technicians ten minutes out." He cautiously approached people and announced the area was now closed due to a mechanical failure. Other security personnel quickly arrived and helped usher the people, many complaining, from the court.

The announcement, saying the food court was now closed and would reopen as soon as it was deemed safe, blared through the ceiling speaker. The message urged everyone to evacuate the area quietly. It took security personnel several minutes to confirm the area was clear. After that, no one approached the closed pop stand.

Lucy and Schuyler stayed behind the curtain, listening. Then, farther down the aisle, the squealing of the accordion fence told them the food court was blocked and locked. They were trapped inside with a daemon lurking somewhere in the shadows.

Large banks of lights began blinking off, leaving the area dark and littered with menacing undertones. The potted trees were freakish shadow forms in the dining section.

"What do we do now?" whispered Schuyler, fingering her bracelet. The pale cheeks under her wide hazel-green eyes revealed her nervousness. Lucy knew how Schuyler felt. She was anxious too.

"Now we wait," said Lucy. "But I don't think we will have to wait long. I have a bad feeling Furfurcas is going to cause a lot of trouble." She grimaced and lifted a shoulder, then went back to peering through the slit.

"This place gives me the creeps. It's like it's a dead zone or something. Yuck," said Schuyler, nervously peering around the supply room. Empty syrup canisters lay scattered on the floor, along with other litter, and the barren shelves looked eerily frightening in the shadowy room. She stayed close to the curtain, not daring to venture farther in.

"I think it's clear. Spectrescope, seal this end of the mall, please." The scope vibrated in Lucy's hand and magically secured the area, sealing it off from the rest of the mall. She put a thumb up. Schuyler nodded.

"Let's go scope the area and see if we can find that daemon," said Lucy, slipping through the curtain and past the fence. She motioned for Schuyler to follow.

"Are you sure no one will see us snooping around?" Schuyler stepped into the eating section, stopped, and listened intently. Out in the main aisleway, excited voices and the tromping of dozens of feet indicated the shoppers were unaware of the danger as they passed the accordion fence.

"Positive. The Spectrescope hasn't failed me yet," said Lucy, glancing toward the excited voices on the other side of the fencing. The brightly colored food vendor marquees and the empty dining tables added an ominous feel to the dimness.

They wandered between the tables, listening and watching for the daemon Santa. It was utterly too quiet. Then Lucy's skin began to prickle.

Eerie laughter bubbled and echoed through the cavernous space, growing louder by the moment. Finally, movement at Buffalo Bill's caught Lucy's eye. The soda dispenser levers began clicking up and down. Red gaseous clouds streamed from each nozzle, spilling over the reservoir and down the front of the machine. Suddenly, every pop station in the food court began emitting the red vapors, wafting throughout the space. The toxic clouds, hazing the area, stank of sulfur. The Spectrescope revealed the ghost. Furfurcas stood nearby, watching and grinning.

Lucy gagged, and Schuyler turned green. The ghost laughed heartily at his prank. The fur pouf on the tip of his hat bounced up and down with the motion. His gray, woolly hair stuck out from under his hat, blending with the dismal gray of his beard. His rosy cheeks were at odds with his glittering black eyes. The daemon pulled back his velvet cloak and placed his hands on his hips. Sucking in a deep breath, he leaned forward, then blew it out.

Suddenly, tables and chairs, litter, napkins, and discarded paper cups tumbled in a whirl toward the unsuspecting girls, still wearing their street clothes. They dove in opposite directions and yelled in unison, "ARMOR!" The hats, vests, and bracelets they wore immediately transmuted into their armor. They tumbled, rolled, and regained their feet. Schuyler unsheathed the Zazriel sword. Lucy still held tight to the magical Spectrescope. "REVEAL!" she shouted.

Furfurcas laughed, not realizing he was visible. The last time he had fought them, he had gotten cleanly away. They'd been no match for a daemon of his rank. He swung his arms, hands cupped to catch air, and jettisoned great blasts of air at them.

The stinky missiles struck their shields, the force pushing them in different directions as their feet slid on the tiles. Lucy felt as though she were standing behind a plane's jet engines, her cheeks rippling as the air tore over the edge of the shield. Schuyler, as she slid past a support column, wrapped an arm and a leg around it, gripping it tightly. Tables and chairs tumbled past and piled up against an invisible barrier. A marquee ripped from the walls, sparks flying, and hurtled past Lucy.

"Spectrescope! I need the Belt of Truth!" shouted Lucy. She felt the belt settle around her waist. If she could get to a stone, she could end this debacle. The gemstones in the belt contained immense power and, combined with the word of the High King, could defeat and conquer every ghost, spirit, and daemon and restore things to normal. But she had to read the inscription and toss the stone for the power to be released. She dropped the Spectrescope into the empty scabbard that was part of the armor at her waist.

Finally, the daemon ran out of breath, and the tumult ceased while he surveyed the damage. A stone wiggled loose from the Belt of Truth, and Lucy caught it in her hand. The inscription appeared inside the glowing stone. "*The face of the High King is against evildoers. He will cut off the memory of them from the earth!*" shouted Lucy, and she threw the stone. It sailed through the air but was caught by another blast. It was pulverized before reaching the daemon.

Lucy stared in disbelief.

The daemon stared in disbelief. He'd just realized he was fully visible.

Furfurcas glowered at Lucy and blew harder this time. His cheeks puffed, and his pink lips formed a circle as he pushed the unseen missile toward Lucy. The blast hit the shield and sent her tumbling toward a pile of debris. Table and chair legs stuck out like weapons as she rolled closer. Schuyler screamed, powerless to help her friend.

With a jerk, Lucy's shield caught the edge of a pastry display case, and though she nearly dislocated her shoulder, it stopped her tumbling. She squirmed around the counter and hid behind the case. Shrugging out of the backpack, she stashed it in a corner, then rubbed her bruised muscle.

"Spirit Sword! I need you!" Immediately the Spectrescope head retreated, and the ethereal blue metal flowed up from the handle. Lucy stood quickly, pointed it, and sent an energy blast into the debris, reducing it to an ashy rumble. Schuyler rushed to Lucy as the tumult died down.

Furfurcas, grinning and apparently amused at the weak little warriors, turned toward the food vendor stands and raised his hands. He chuckled as display cases exploded, shards of glass flying everywhere. Food flew about the court; french fries, burgers, and buns plastered the floors, walls, and ceiling. Soft-serve ice cream oozed from dispensers, dribbling down the machine fronts and puddling on the floor. Ketchup and mustard bottles exploded their contents into the air. At the Chinese takeout stand, rice showered down like confetti. Containers of kung pao chicken blew up and drenched the girls in a sticky, spicy sauce.

Next came the marquees crashing to the floor, the bare electrical wires swinging dangerously and sparking like fireworks. Ceiling tiles fell, breaking against the floor with plumes of dust, and the Christmas ornaments shattered, tiny shards littering the floor like multicolored glitter around the toppled trees.

"Lucy, what are we going to do? We've never encountered such a strong spirit before!" Schuyler knelt beside Lucy behind the case as the daemon gleefully obliterated Christmas.

"Don't worry; we'll be fine. We'll show this ghost a thing or two," Lucy growled, staring down the court at the ghost. As Furfurcas flung his arms about, objects tossed themselves against the walls and floors.

Stomping toward the daemon, Lucy held the Spirit Sword above her head. "Furfurcas! In the name of the High King, you must tell me your daemon name!" Blood trickled down her cheek from a deep gash. Dirt and grease smeared her breastplate, and the helmet dripped with sauce.

The daemon grinned and placed his hands over his ears. "La la la la la," he chanted. "I can't hear you! You have no power over me, human."

Lucy flattened her lips and glared at the daemon. Her gaze darted across the oozing ice cream as it streamed from the tap, and an idea formed. She cupped her hand and swiped it toward the spirit. The ghost was hit with a giant blob of soft-serve chocolate ice cream, the concoction splattering his face and beard. She twisted her hand and aimed the spicket at the daemon, spewing its chocolatey confection and covering the ghost like a giant ice cream cone.

"Oh, good one, Lucy!" shouted Schuyler, doing a fist pump and giggling.

Furfurcas wiped a beefy hand across his face, flinging the sticky remnants aside. This time, he grabbed a cement bench from the commons area and flung it. Lucy ducked behind a section of booths; Schuyler yelped and dove behind Lucy as the bench smashed to pieces on the floor where they had been standing.

"Schuyler, stand with me. We'll point our swords at him and blast him with energy. Be sure to lean into it and brace your feet. The stream will be strong. Once we have him down, we can hit him with a stone."

"Got it!" said Schuyler decisively, though her eyes, like huge orbs in her pale cheeks, belied her confidence. Her face was surrounded by a mass of messy and dispirited blonde curls hanging from under her helmet.

"Now! Blast that daemon!" shouted Lucy. Energy beams burst from the ends of their swords and engulfed the daemon. The daemon, trusting in his superiority, struggled to regain control. The blast consumed the cream and singed his hair, his cloak, and his hat. Even his boots smoldered. Pushing against the energy beam, he gained a fraction of space, barely keeping the blast back.

A broken marquee lay nearby. Lucy pointed her hand at it, then whipped her arm forward. The marquee shot into the air and sped toward the ghost.

The ghost flung an arm sideways, and the marquee smashed into a wall, splintering into shrapnel. The spirit levitated a large potted plant in a cement container and threw it at them.

"Freeze!" yelled Lucy. The heavy object hung in midair. She swiped her hand, and the plant drifted away.

Still deflecting the blast, the daemon waggled his eyebrows. Then, smirking, he winked and disappeared with a pop.

The beams dissipated, and the girls dropped their swords, exhausted and discouraged. Twice now, their encounters with the daemon had left them defeated and the daemon still on the loose. Glancing at each other, each knowing the disappointment the other felt, they turned and surveyed the damage. The food court was in ruins and stank of sulfur and burned sugars.

"Oh, Luce. I hope the stones can help fix all this damage—and quick. If anyone finds us here, we're going to be blamed and jailed for sure." Schuyler whimpered as she saw all the damage to Buffalo Bill's Burger stand. "Aw! After all this, I don't think I'll ever be able to eat another Buffalo Bill burger again. Or a chocolate shake."

Two white stones wiggled loose and popped into Lucy's hand. After reading the inscriptions, she snickered and poked Schuyler in the shoulder. "Don't worry, girlfriend. The High King has this covered. '*Do not worry about what you will eat or what you will drink. Is not life more than food?*' " Schuyler rolled her lips and looked at the ceiling.

"Come on, we better get this done," said Lucy. "*The High King hears and will deliver you out of all your troubles. He will renew the ruined places. Wait for my renewal to come.*"

She threw the stone.

Sleep Is Overrated

6

"Grandma! You're here!" shouted Lucy, rushing forward, grabbing the septuagenarian lady, and nearly knocking them both to the floor. Recovering quickly, Lucy pulled her grandma around in a whirl, making her grandma giggle like a schoolgirl, face flushed.

"My goodness! Give an old lady a chance to catch her breath," said Grandma Elliot, laughing and hugging her granddaughter. Then, releasing the girl, she leaned back and lovingly surveyed the growing, rosy-cheeked teenager whose gray eyes sparkled with mischievousness. Lucy must have grown at least an inch or more since Thanksgiving.

"Oh, you look so adorable. Vivian's excellent food offerings and wonderful care agree with you." Grandma Elliot leaned in for another quick hug.

The smile dropped from Jeannie's face, who was waiting her turn to greet her mother. A single eyebrow raised, and her lips puckered. Then she threw her hands up, stepped away, and took a deep breath.

"And of course, I'm not doing such a bang-up job, am I, Mother? Is that what you're saying?" Jeannie demanded, crossing her arms.

"I'm not saying anything of the kind," said Grandma Elliot. "Jeannie, you're under a tremendous amount of stress just now, and the McGoos are taking wonderful care of all of you. That's all I'm saying. And I, for one, am grateful to them," she said, pulling her daughter into a hug. "Goodness, I haven't been in the house five minutes. It's going to be a long visit if we keep at each other. Truce?"

Reluctantly, Jeannie returned the hug, although not nearly as loving as her mother's. Then, nodding her agreement, she stepped back and reached for the wheeled suitcase sitting beside the front door. "You will be sharing Lucy's room; Vivian has made up the bed near the window for you. I'll take this upstairs for you to unpack later." Dragging the suitcase behind, Jeannie disappeared down the hall and lugged it up the staircase.

"Lucy, why don't you come help me unload the Christmas presents? It will give your mom a little time to cool down." Grandma Elliot tugged her gloves back on and headed outside to the truck.

"Wow! Grandma, this is so cool," exclaimed Lucy, staring at the red 1948 Chevy pickup with big, rounded fenders, black running boards, and chrome trims sitting in the driveway. "I didn't know you drove a pickup." She walked all around the vehicle, admiring the red wheels with their shiny chrome center hubcaps. "When did you get it?" She ran a hand lightly over the tailgate of the boxy truck bed.

"It was your granddad's," said Grandma Elliot, her eyes misting. "He finished the restoration shortly before he passed on. A friend has a huge garage to showcase his antique automobiles, and he has been storing the truck for me and keeping it in good running order. He and your granddad were close friends since their high school days."

She pressed a gloved finger to her nose, sniffled, then smiled. "Sorry, dear. It's been years, but I still miss your granddad. Driving it makes me feel closer to him, and it just seemed appropriate. Your granddad enjoyed delivering presents to the neighborhood kids and those less fortunate."

"You're not lonely, are you, Grandma?" asked Lucy, unlatching the tailgate and crawling into the truck bed. The gifts nestled inside cardboard boxes that were strapped to its sides. "How did you get these in here?"

Grandma Elliot giggled. "Oh, that would be a Harold thing. He's the friend with the garage. He didn't want them rolling about the back as I drove. He's very thoughtful that way." She reached for the box Lucy shoved toward the tailgate.

"Let me help you with those, Mrs. Elliot," said Mr. Bill, rushing to help. "Me and my bad manners. Vivian will have my hide when she finds out. She's in the kitchen prepping for dinner. Sundays, we always have fried chicken, corn bread, and grits. Viv's a bit of a southern girl at heart." He hefted the box into his arms and smiled. "It's good to see you again, Leona," he called over his shoulder as he headed inside.

"So, are you lonely, Grandma?" asked Lucy again, tugging at the other box.

"Sometimes, now that Isabel has passed on. The house is a little too quiet at times. But I'm not complaining. Since Isabel left the house to me, I may sell it and get something smaller, but with plenty of bedrooms so you can all come to visit." She winked at Lucy.

"Ooh, that should go well, especially with grumpy Mom in there," said Lucy, thumbing at the house. "Why are you two always snarking at each other? I don't understand." She sat cross-legged on the tailgate and waited for her grandma to answer. The lady smiled wryly and glanced at her boots.

"I can only say this: it's not my story to tell. Maybe someday your *grumpy mom* will tell you. But for now, let's get the rest of these gifts inside. It's not getting any warmer out here. It is December, after all."

The Ghost Writer

The Spectrescope vibrated under her pillow. Lucy had slept with the artifact since discovering that the daemon ghost, Furfurcas, wasn't bound to haunting the school. The rune symbols on the ring under the magnifying head were glowing and transforming, and the handle was getting warm. It was disconcerting since that almost always meant something bad was about to happen.

Quickly dressing, she eased open the bedroom door, careful not to wake her grandma snoring in the other bed. *Boy, things sure get complicated*, she thought. She gently closed the door and tiptoed down the hallway and the stairs.

The Christmas tree in the corner of the living room was still lit and twinkling. It brought a smile to Lucy's face; she loved Christmas, and this dumb ghost was playing havoc with her happy holidays. Next, the dining room appeared normal, and the kitchen, with its wonderful aromas still lingering, was undisturbed. The McGoos' room was at the back of the house, down the short hallway from the kitchen and dinette. The vicinity was quiet. She didn't want to disturb them unless she had to; she should be able to handle this on her own.

A noise from the living room made her turn back. Sneaking through the connecting dining room, she slid along the wall, then peeked around the corner. Fully visible, the daemon ghost was riffling through the presents under the tree, ripping the paper from the gifts and smashing the contents.

Lucy gripped the Spectrescope and silently uttered her request. The room took on a muffled quality, as though a giant bubble had settled over it, dampening the sound and protecting the space. The daemon, noticing the change, stiffened and glanced about the room. Taking a deep breath, Lucy stepped around the corner. Her clothing had transformed; she was wearing her armor. She raised her shield.

"Furfurcas! In the name of the High—"

The daemon swung his hand and lobbed a fiery projectile at her. Lucy ducked, the blazing fireball hitting her shield and flaring out. ". . . King! Tell me your—" A fireball slammed her shield. "Ooh!" said Lucy, stamping her foot. The daemon threw another fireball.

She raised her hand and yelled, "FREEZE!" The fireball stopped dead, hanging in midair. Lucy whipped her hand and hurtled it at the spirit. Furfurcas ducked. The missile smacked the Christmas tree instead. The live evergreen tree burst into flames, the fire licking the ceiling. The rest of the house was free from the danger, but the tree was quickly reducing to ashes.

"Holy cow!" said Lucy, staring in disbelief at the inferno. The daemon forgotten, Lucy rushed forward, her heart pounding. "Help! Spectrescope, *do* something!"

The magical artifact vibrated in her hand. The message in the lens said, *Extinguish and restore.* She dropped her head, duly reprimanded.

With one hand holding the scope, she raised the other and commanded, "EXTINGUISH." The flames disappeared with a pop and a swoosh, taking the acrid stench of burned pine resin with them. Once the flames were out, she repeated the process and commanded, "RESTORE." The room, the gifts, and the charming Christmas tree with its lights and vintage decorations reappeared. With the room cleaned and back to normal, Lucy sighed with relief as her shoulders slumped.

And then her head whipped up as she remembered the ghost.

Just then, a car engine rumbled and caught her attention. *No!* she thought, rushing to the windows and yanking back the curtains. The ghost was sitting in her grandma's vintage red pickup truck, smiling gleefully. He rolled the window down and waved, then backed out of the driveway.

Lucy threw open the front door and chased after the ghost driving the truck down the dark, empty street. "FREEZE! FREEZE! FREEZE!" she screamed, then cringed, hoping she hadn't awakened the neighbors. She shook her head, frazzled and overwhelmed at her stupidity and arrogance. She should have asked the McGoos for their help. They were guardian spirits. The truck halted, its tires spinning on the snowy pavement as if set on a treadmill. The wheels spun, but the pickup wasn't going anywhere.

The ghost was trapped in the truck, pushing against the door, but he couldn't get out. Lucy trudged through the snow to the vehicle and glared at the apparition, who was now sitting calmly and twirling the pouf of fur on the tip of his hat. His soulless black eyes belied his portrayal of a jolly ole soul. He draped his arm out the window and tapped his fingertips against the door.

"You are a pain in my backside," growled Lucy, staring at the ghost. The Spectrescope head had retreated, and she now held the Spirit Sword pointed at the daemon. He looked at the pointy tip held mere inches from his nose and smiled. Not exactly the reaction Lucy expected. A quiver of fear from the daemon would have bolstered her confidence.

"Furfurcas, in the name of the High King, you must tell me your daemon name!" she commanded, circling the tip of the sword. Her armor gleamed under the streetlights. She observed him as he considered the emblem on the front of her shield. His eyes narrowed.

The shield's crest was a white fox holding a flag embellished with a sword, a golden cross, and a crown. The crest angered the daemon, his eyes glittering dangerously. His gaze slipped from the shield to look directly into Lucy's clear gray eyes. He smiled benignly.

"Why, certainly, dear lady," said Furfurcas, tipping his head. "My real name is Confusion, though it won't mean much to your small human brain. You have little understanding of the real world," he said, slowly shaking his head. "You are so typical of your species. You only believe what you can see. Yet, what is invisible is so much more real than what you can see. There is another existence, one with the power to grant you the deepest desires of your heart. You would clearly see if you opened your eyes. But unfortunately, your High King would keep you from it. I can help you; you know I can."

Lucy stared at the daemon. She heard the words coming from his mouth, but she was suddenly so tired, she wanted only to go back to bed and let the world go on as it would. The Spirit Sword began to waver, dipping as she held it, still pointed at the smiling daemon in her grandma's truck. *Why am I pointing a sword at Santa?* thought Lucy. *Huh.*

The ghost smiled kindly, noticing the sleepy, drooping eyelids. The hand tapping the door panel suddenly came up, deflecting the sword point away. The contact with the Spirit Sword burned his hand, the stench quickly roiling upward. He yelped.

Lucy coughed and gagged and came to her senses. She brought the sword up but not before the spirit reacted.

The daemon shoved open the door, slamming it into her shield and knocking her down. The Spirit Sword skittered away through the snow. Furfurcas lunged from the truck and darted down the street, back to the house, and up the porch steps.

Lucy scrabbled for the sword, grabbed it, and chased the ghost back to the McGoos' house and into the living room. She saw his feet disappearing up the stairs and ran after him.

At the top of the stairs, she halted and gaped in wonder.

A golden-haired entity dressed in a flowing blue gown was grappling with the velvet-clad Santa daemon. The angelic entity stood her ground in front of Jeanie Hornberger's bedroom door.

"Depart, Furfurcas! You have no business here. In the name of the High King, *depart*, I say!" uttered the beautiful lady.

"Oh, Helena, you know better than I how ridiculous that sounds. The woman will be ours. All she needs to do is complete her turning," said Furfurcas. "Even now, she is close to deciding."

"You must leave, Furfurcas. You will not be successful. She has the promise of the High King. She only needs to remember."

"Yes, but if I can get her to deny the High King, she will be ours forever," growled Furfurcas.

"Depart from here, evil one," said Helena, her glowing countenance radiating its light to the hallway. Her arms spread to each side, and she blocked the daemon from entering the bedroom.

The staff he usually carried had been absent earlier, but now it appeared in his hand. The club end of it bounced menacingly in his palm. His black eyes flashed as he considered the angelic entity. He raised the club over his head slowly. "Too bad for you," he said.

Just then, two white winged creatures surged up the stairs. The rapid beating of their wings displaced the air around Furfurcas, confusing him. They darted about the daemon, whispering. Then, while not touching him, they thrust him about like a limp noodle. On the hat tip, the pouf of fur whipped about like a Ping-Pong ball, slapping him in the face.

Then he saw Lucy standing at the top of the stairs, holding the Spirit Sword. There were too many obstacles to his mission tonight. He growled, and with a hiss and a pop, he disappeared.

Jeannie crawled into bed, exhausted from another day of pounding the computer keys. Even as she sent inquiries to online job postings, she fully expected to be told that her skill set didn't match anything the companies were looking to hire. At this point, even a greeter position at the local hypermarket would help. While the McGoos were kind and hospitable, she couldn't imagine them being patient with her much longer, and she didn't want to be a burden. Her mistakes were her own, and she needed to fix things. And somehow, she needed to fix things with her mother, at least for the time being, so they could get through the holidays in one piece. Bickering with her mother never resolved anything.

The face in the bathroom mirror tonight belonged to someone else. The once-round cheeks had sunken, the rosy bloom had faded, and lines were encasing her eyes. The few clothes she had purchased after the fire now hung loosely on her frame, and her hair was in dire need of a cut and style. *Maybe a good night's sleep will help. Things will look brighter in the morning*, Jeannie thought. She placed the bottle of the all-natural sleep aid from the health food store on the nightstand, turned off the light, and burrowed into the covers. Finally, she closed her eyes and eventually drifted off to sleep.

When she opened her eyes again, the dark bedroom felt different somehow. Warily, she sat up and glanced around. Everything appeared normal; the ambient light from the windows still cast its pale beam on the wall, the clock on the nightstand ticked off the seconds, and the pale presence of the night-light in the hall showed itself under the edge of the door.

At least she thought it was the night-light—until the doorknob creaked and began to turn.

"Oh, not again," whispered Jeannie, preparing to dive under the covers as the door eased itself open.

Slam!

The door suddenly banged shut. Jeannie heard a scuffle and muffled voices on the other side of the door. More curious than afraid this time, she slowly rose, slipped into her robe and slippers, and crept to the door. Easing the door open a crack, she peered out. Her hand flew to her mouth, stifling a yelp.

There, in the hallway, two opaque spirits were pushing each other. The tall, regal, light-emitting ghost with the long golden hair was arguing with a large burly entity wrapped in a red-velvet cloak and wearing a fur-trimmed hat. He looked very much like an angry mall Santa.

Suddenly, two white winged creatures flew up the staircase, chirping and chattering at the Santa ghost and knocking him about with their wings. They appeared too much for the Santa ghost, and he disappeared with a pop. Then the winged entities, as tall and shapely as humans, spoke with the golden entity. Their wings had folded and disappeared behind their backs. Their words were indistinct and whispered quickly.

Confused and unsure what she was seeing, Jeannie eased the door open further, hoping to glimpse the entities' faces and hear the conversation. The door creaked. Helena quickly faded away while the other two entities spun toward her, resuming their human identities. She gasped and fainted, her body falling unhindered in a heap to the floor.

"Uh-oh," said Bill.

"Help me get her back to bed," said Vivian, "then when she wakes up, she'll think it was dream."

"Well, that's one story, Viv."

"And I'm sticking to it," said Vivian, marching toward the bedroom door.

A Busy Evening

7

"Thanks for dinner, Ms. Vivian," said Lucy, placing the dirty plates in the dishwasher as Schuyler piled them on the counter. "You should let me make the dinner sometime. It isn't fair that you should do all the cooking." She shut the dishwasher and set it to run.

"Oh, it's not a problem, dearie. I am enjoying every minute with you and your family. It's no trouble at all," said Vivian. Flour dusted her apron as she stirred the batter she was preparing. A container of buttermilk, along with a pint of blueberries, sat on the counter. Flour dusted them too.

"What are you making this late?" asked Lucy. She got a spoon from the drawer, dipped it into the batter, and tasted it. "Oh! That's yummy."

"These are my buttermilk blueberry muffins. I'll bake them before bed, let them cool overnight, and then drizzle a warm lemon glaze over them in the morning." Vivian added the prepared blueberries and folded them into the batter, careful not to squash the berries. "Scrambled eggs and bacon will taste wonderful next to the sweet-tart flavors from the muffins."

"That's why your house always smells so good!" said Schuyler. "My mouth is watering just thinking about them. Even the batter smells yummy!" She leaned close and wafted the air toward her nose. "I can't wait for breakfast. Can I stay till Christmas?"

"You can if you like," said Vivian, smiling.

"Don't encourage her, Ms. Vivian. She'll do it too," said Lucy, who promptly received a jab in the shoulder. Schuyler poked her tongue out. Vivian snickered.

"Oh, it is good to have youngsters in the house. You make it so lively." Vivian smiled and portioned the batter into the prepared muffin tin. "If you're both still awake later when these finish baking, I'll let you know. They taste just as good with a dollop of butter on top, all melty and oozing into the texture."

Lucy reached past Ms. Vivian, grabbed a napkin, and handed it to Schuyler. "Here, use this. You're drooling." Vivian burst out laughing, dabbing her eyes with the corner of her apron. Schuyler snatched the napkin, squinting and scrunching her nose at Lucy.

"Come along, Cookie Monster, we have work to do," said Lucy, waving at her friend to follow as she headed for the stairs. "And Schuyler? Thanks for staying overnight."

Mr. Bill relaxed in the living room with his feet propped up on the blue-and-white ottoman. He got up when he spotted them and hurried to the foot of the stairs.

"Lucy, I need to speak to you and Schuyler," he whispered. The girls stopped and waited.

He glanced about and saw Jeannie using the computer in the dining room. Lucy's grandma, Leona, was reading in the living room. Dale had already disappeared to his bedroom.

"I have a feeling something big may happen tonight," he whispered. "The Furfurcas daemon is a powerful spirit. You will need help. Vivian and I will be here. We'll do what we can, but if we can't come to you, don't forget to use the power of the artifacts, and be sure to wear all your armor." He tapped the side of his nose, winked, and returned to the living room.

"Okay then. Good talk," whispered Lucy, and she headed upstairs to the guest room. Entering the room, she smiled. Ms. Vivian had already made up a bed for Schuyler. An inflatable mattress was lying next to Lucy's bed and wrapped with colorful sheets, blankets, and extra pillows. A clean set of towels sat on the foot of the makeshift bed.

"Wow. Ms. Vivian thinks of everything," said Schuyler with a snicker. "I may have to move in here with you. Not to mention the free access to the pantry and all the chocolate chip cookies I can eat. It's almost heaven!" She laughed, dropped her overnight case in the corner, and plopped down on the mattress.

"Okay, here's the plan," said Lucy, ignoring Schuyler's comments. She sat cross-legged on her bed. "We'll have to be careful not to wake Grandma. She sleeps rather soundly and snores a lot, but still, I don't want her to come to any harm."

"Can you ask the Spectrescope to seal the room to protect her?" asked Schuyler, laying out her hat and vest. She was wearing the bracelet.

Lucy raised an eyebrow and considered the request. "I don't honestly know, but it's worth trying." She got the scope from the backpack and held it. "Spectrescope, could you seal the room to protect Grandma Elliot when we leave?" The scope grew warm in her hands, and then after a moment, a message appeared in the lens. *Grandma Elliot is protected.* Lucy grinned and nodded at Schuyler. "Easy peasy, girlfriend. Now, if we can only dispense with that daemon, we might get a merry Christmas after all."

Schuyler nodded sagely and crawled beneath the covers on her mattress. "Have you asked Iam, the High King, about these ghosts?" She popped a stick of gum and chewed.

"I've been calling him, but he hasn't answered or shown up or anything. So now I wonder if I did something to offend him." Lucy now knew that Iam, the vendor from the flea market who had sold her the trunk with the artifacts, was really the High King of Ascalon, and she had come to love him dearly.

"Iam never does anything without reason. Maybe he's letting you figure this one out by yourself." Schuyler fell back on the pillows and twirled a lock of hair.

"Maybe you're right, but this is the strongest entity we've encountered yet," said Lucy. "I could use his input on this. We do have the McGoos to help, though, and that's some comfort."

"So, what happened last night? You've been a little weird all day," said Schuyler. "You hardly said anything at school today."

"I nearly set the house on fire," said Lucy, hanging her head.

"What? How?" Schuyler popped another stick of gum in her mouth and chewed rapidly.

"After everyone went to bed, Furfurcas showed up. He lobbed a fireball at me, and I shot it back at him, but it lodged in the Christmas tree." Lucy's chin fell to her chest. "He disappeared, and the tree went up in flames, scorching the ceiling. Then Furfurcas stole grandma's red truck and took off down the street. I had to tell Mr. Bill what happened, and he retrieved the truck."

"Wowza. You did have a bad night. I should have been here to help you."

"We didn't do so well at the mall if you remember correctly," said Lucy, still pouting.

"And I remember we survived to fight another day. We didn't do so bad, girlfriend," said Schuyler. She pulled a stick of gum from the pack and waggled it.

"You and food," said Lucy, taking the gum, her eyes rolling in circles.

"Technically, the gum isn't a food. It's something I chew when I get nervous," said Schuler, popping more gum in her mouth, her cheek bulging like a chipmunk.

Lucy snorted, then laughed. It felt good to laugh.

Burp. Burp. Burrrrrp.

"What?" asked Lucy, sitting up and yawning. She stretched her arms over her head.

Burp. Burp. Burrrrrp.

"Schuyler!" whispered Lucy, leaning over the edge of the bed and poking Schuyler in the head. "It's time to go. The Spectrescope activated, and the runes are morphing." She crawled quietly to the foot of the bed and carefully eased her feet to the floor. A glance told her Grandma Elliot was sleeping peacefully.

Lucy frowned. The vest was wrinkled from wearing it to bed, as was the floppy hat. Her jeans hadn't fared much better; they were wrinkled too. Nevertheless, she nervously twirled the bracelet around her wrist. The Belt of Truth ring twinkled on her finger.

Schuyler sat up, yawned, and shook her head, flipping her blonde curls. She slipped her shoes on and tiptoed to the door and waited.

Lucy scowled at her. "Why aren't your clothes wrinkled? I look like I slept in the dryer," she grumbled, easing the door open and checking the hallway before proceeding. It was clear.

"I straightened my clothes when I lay down and pulled as many wrinkles out as I could," whispered Schuyler, smirking. "Try it next time. It works." Lucy squinted at her. "What now, oh wise one?"

"Let's check the house. The Spectrescope alerted me, so Furfurcas must be here somewhere," Lucy said, slowly moving toward the stairs. She got no farther than the top step when she heard a whimper and motioned to Schuyler to wait. The whimper came again. This time she could tell it had come from her mom's room.

"My mom!" mouthed Lucy, pointing down the hall. The Spectrescope vibrated, the runes morphing. First, the Santa image appeared, followed by an angelic rune with a halo and a circle, followed by runes of two girls. Schuyler pointed a finger at the circle image and looked questioningly at Lucy, who shook her head and eased toward the bedroom door.

A pale light was visible under the door, with shadows breaking the beam, moving about. Voices whispered, the words indistinct. The whimpering tore at Lucy. She placed her hand on the doorknob and cracked the door open.

Inside, the golden-haired angelic entity from the other night whispered to her mom, who was crying and shaking her head. Lucy could not hear the words. They were meant for her mom alone. Where the window should have been, there was a spinning circle of light with a sparkling core at its center. It was lovely and disturbing too.

Lucy eased the door open and stepped inside, followed closely by Schuyler. Both girls were speechless. Without acknowledging the girls' presence, the spirit clasped Jeannie's hand, and together they stepped through the spinning circle and disappeared. Lucy gasped; Schuyler's hand flew to her open mouth, her eyes wide.

Before either of them could speak, Furfurcas burst into the room, shoving them aside, and dove for the portal. Instantly, their armor and weapons appeared.

Reacting on instinct alone, Lucy rushed the daemon before he made it to the portal. They both crashed to the floor as she wrapped her arms around his legs. "Spectrescope, seal this room!" shouted Lucy.

Immediately the atmosphere changed, taking on a quality of shimmering warmth that moved in waves like heat across hot pavement. Schuyler pulled the Zazriel sword from its sheath and hurried forward. Lucy and Furfurcas rolled about, pounding each other. With Lucy's arm still wrapped around his legs, the daemon couldn't stand, but his weight had her trapped. So, he conjured his staff and swung.

The club end slammed into Lucy's shield, the force reverberating painfully through her arm. Still, she clung to the daemon. He grappled and crawled his way closer to the portal. He had to stop Helena. If he stopped her, his mission would be successful.

Schuyler landed multiple hits on the daemon, but each strike was deflected as though a forcefield protected him. Finally, the spirit was nearing the portal. He pulled a leg free and violently kicked Lucy in the head. The helmet took most of the impact, but his boot heel broke her nose.

The force rattled her senses. Blood dripped into her mouth, and she gagged and spit. Then, her grip loosened, and the daemon was free. He hurried to his feet, stood, and swiped his arm through the air. The bed rose, flipped, and landed on both girls, knocking them down and trapping them underneath. Furfurcas laughed, the sound booming in the confines of the room. The portal was still active, the light spinning around inside the circle.

He dove through the portal.

A Whale of a Good Time

"Spectrescope, help, please!" whimpered Lucy from under the bed. She could hear Schuyler somewhere close by in the dark and called out to her.

"Schuyler, are you okay? Where are you?" The bed levitated, turned right side up, and hovered as they crawled from underneath it. Finally, the bed settled into its usual place, and the covers were tucked and smoothed by unseen hands. The room was otherwise unscathed.

Lucy reached a hand to Schuyler and pulled her up. They were shaken but unhurt by the brief and robust fight with the daemon, except for Lucy's broken nose. She dabbed the blood on her shirtsleeve.

"C'mon! We're going through the portal," said Lucy, grabbing Schuyler's hand and running at the spinning wheel. "Jump!"

As soon as they went through the circle of light, they were caught in a vortex, spinning out of control and tumbling through space that wasn't space; it felt like a void with no sound and no light, and then it spat them out.

They landed with a crash on the cold black-and-white marble tiles in a cavernous space. Rolling to their backs, they lay there for a moment to catch their breaths, chests heaving. Lucy opened her eyes first, looked up, and screamed at the top of her lungs. Schuyler's scream soon joined hers as they looked up through the milky-white bones of a whale skeleton hanging directly above their heads and swinging on its wires.

Disoriented, Schuyler scrambled to her feet and tried to run in several directions at the same time. Finally, she fell to her knees next to Lucy, who was still lying on the floor, staring at the skeleton. The temperature wasn't cold, but she wrapped her arms around herself and concentrated on taking deep breaths to clear the brain fog from her head. It helped a little.

Lucy blinked several times and let her unfocused gaze roam about the space as her mind tried to fit the puzzle pieces together. After the tumble through the space-time vortex, her brain felt like mush. Finally, she sat up and looked around, and her vision slowly cleared.

On either side of her, a broad white staircase led to a second-floor balcony that encompassed the entire space. The concave ceiling glowed with ethereal light and brightened the whole room, for that was what it was—a giant white room.

Behind them, in the center of the cavernous room, sat an information desk, curving around until it formed a perfect U shape, complete with pamphlets, maps, and a telephone. On the other side of the information desk sat a grouping of mammoth elephants, their footprints embedded in the sand behind them. Along the walls were benches.

The walls held what appeared to be miniature portals, each allowing the viewer a glimpse a different time and place. Some gateways kept animals, and others had buildings and little people. Everything was motionless and still.

Lucy stared at each of the time portals, her brain working to understand why everything seemed familiar and yet wasn't. Finally, she stood, went to one, and looked inside. The landscape was beautiful, the blue sky was nearly cloudless, and a family of deer peacefully grazed, unaware of being frozen in time.

The next gateway was a tundra of rolling blue-white hills against a brilliant blue sky. Footprints in the snow led to a pack of timber wolves huddled together under an evergreen tree.

The brain fog began to lift while she gazed at the scene. *It's not a portal*, she thought. *It's a diorama.* She pressed a button on the wall, and a deep, soothing voice spoke, telling the story of the depicted scene. *The museum!*

"Schuyler! I know *where* we are, but I don't know *when* we are." Lucy walked back to Schuyler and yanked her to her feet. "I think this is the old museum. It was closed decades ago. I've only seen photos of it, but it looks like the same place. Only it's not abandoned yet in this time."

"Wowza. My head is fuzzy," said Schuyler, shaking her head and blinking. "It does look like a museum. Are those the same whale bones as in the new museum?" Tilting her head back, she gazed at the skeleton. "So cool. Maybe you could borrow this one for Mr. Bulman's classroom," she said, smirking. "Think we could get it back through the portal?"

"Ha ha. I think you bumped your head on something when we went through the vortex," said Lucy.

"So, what are we doing in an old, abandoned museum? Do you think your mom and the daemon are here some-where too?" She glanced at her clothes, then remembered they had been wearing armor when they went through the portal. "Lucy! Our armor changed."

"I wonder if the vortex had something to do with it," said Lucy. "We're still wearing the magical clothes, and we have our bracelets."

"But Lucy, where is the Spectrescope?" asked Schuyler, a hand on her chest, her eyes wide.

"Oh, holy cow! I don't know where it is! I had it when we went through the portal. It must be here somewhere. It just has to be!" Frantically, she searched along the floor, under the benches, and behind the information desk. It wasn't in any of those places.

Schuyler cautiously explored the exits off the main floor that led to other rooms and various displays. The Spectrescope wasn't in any place she searched, so she went back to the enormous room and found Lucy rifling through the cabinets and drawers that comprised the large information desk.

"Did you find it? Please tell me that you found it," said Lucy, her voice muffled. She was sitting on the floor with tissues stuffed up her bleeding nose and a box of tissues next to her.

Resisting a snarky comment, Schuyler shook her head instead. "Sorry, I got nothing, girlfriend." She glanced around the room again, then up at the whale bones. "Uh, Lucy?"

"Yeah?" A perplexed look on her face, Lucy followed Schuyler's gaze and looked up. "Oh, you've got to be kidding me!" Then, jumping to her feet, hands on hips, she glared at the offensive whale bones and grunted.

Stuck between the ribs was the Spectrescope.

Lucy scratched her head and craned her neck as she walked beneath the structure, looking for a possible way to retrieve the scope. "All this looking up has blood running down my throat. Gross."

"What do we do now?" asked Schuyler, chewing at a hangnail and sitting cross-legged on the information desk.

"Well, hello. Whatever are you looking at, I wonder?" asked a familiar, unfriendly voice. "You look even smaller from this viewpoint, did you know?" Furfurcas said with a laugh.

Lucy and Schuyler whirled around, looking for the daemon. They found him casually resting his arms on the balcony railing on the second floor, fully visible. The smirk on his face was undeniable, his fur pouf swinging as he leaned over the barrier. A brief stench of sulfur wafted down to them. Schuyler wrinkled her nose, waving a hand. Lucy couldn't smell anything through the tissue in her broken nose, but she could taste the sulfur on her tongue.

"Armor!" said Lucy. The bracelet transformed to her shield and spare sword, Ratha-nael, and her armor appeared too. The Belt of Truth settled around her waist along with her spare scabbard. At least she had a weapon. Glancing up at the Spectrescope, she grimaced. She'd worry about that later.

Schuyler jumped off the desk just as her armor morphed, and she withdrew the Zazriel sword. Standing next to Lucy, she looked ready, but Lucy knew she was nervous too.

"What do you want, Furfurcas?" asked Lucy. "Why are you here?" Then, moving slowly toward one of the staircases, she jerked her head and motioned Schuyler to take the other stairs. It wasn't as though the daemon couldn't figure out their strategy from where he was standing. Lucy just hoped one of them could get to the daemon and distract him while the other came from behind and hopefully vanquished him.

"I thought I should have a little chat with your mother. After all, I can be rather persuasive, and she shouldn't listen to all that babble from Helena," said Furfurcas. He grinned, raised his hand, and lobbed several flaming balls at her.

Lucy ducked and threw herself against the steps. The missiles struck the wall and scorched the paint. Sparks rained down on her, burning her unprotected skin. Furfurcas laughed, and the sound echoed through the vast space. She ran up the stairs to the mezzanine over the entrance on the lower floor and slid behind the short wall. The Spectrescope was still dangling from the whale skeleton. *If I could only get to the scope*, thought Lucy, *maybe we could end this.*

The sword in her hand, Ratha-nael, vibrated, startling her. A script flamed along the blade, leaving behind a glowing message that brought a huge smile to her face, and she nearly giggled. It read, *I am Ratha-nael, thwarter of daemons. I can help you, Gatekeeper.* Grinning, she kissed the blade and ran down the balcony toward the daemon.

The spirit growled, the smile falling from his face when he saw she had survived his onslaught. He walked toward her, tossing his flaming grenades one after another until the whole place stank.

Her face grim and determined, she continued advancing toward him, deflecting the flames with her shield or extinguishing them with a slice from the sword. The occasional errant spark scorched her breastplate.

Schuyler dashed up the stairs and gained the upper balcony without the daemon noticing. She crept behind the railing wall toward the spirit. Sensing movement, Furfurcas swung around, pushing the air. The daemon then turned back toward Lucy and continued his assault.

The force hit Schuyler and hurtled her through a diorama. The glass shattered; shards pierced her arms and left her bloodied. The dented helmet left her momentarily dazed and confused and wondering why there were deer staring at her as she slumped against an artificial rock. Then her lungs involuntarily sucked in a deep breath, and her head cleared as she sat up.

Schuyler's sword was on the floor several feet away. She lunged for it, rolling as Furfurcas lobbed another fireball at her. Instead, the fireball hit the diorama, scorching the deer and charring the painted background.

"Schuyler! Get ready," yelled Lucy, slowly advancing on the daemon. By now, she had nearly made it to a junction where a corridor led to more exhibits. Schuyler rolled to her feet with shield and sword ready, her stance firm. "Now!" shouted Lucy.

Simultaneously from two directions, the swords blasted the daemon with a blinding energy beam. The two beams converged into one point. Furfurcas struggled to push against the energy, his arms stiff and hands splayed before him. His arms were shaking from the force of the powerful wave.

"Keep it going," shouted Lucy, continuing toward the spirit. "He's weakening!" Schuyler nodded.

Furfurcas hunched his shoulders, seeming to roll into himself. His head drooped down, and his arms folded to his chest. Then, suddenly, he stood, straightening his arms and deflecting the energy with a blast that sent the whale skeleton erupting from the ceiling.

The explosion rippled in waves and sent bones flying everywhere. They shattered displays, pierced the walls, and ripped tiles from the ceiling. In a millisecond, the cavernous space was rubble. The tusks of the overturned mammoths from the elephant exhibit were embedded in the floor. The large, hairy mammoth legs pointed up, and sand was scattered everywhere. The obliterated information desk and the benches below lay broken and twisted.

Furfurcas turned, unharmed but weakened from their combined strength, and fled farther into the museum.

"Schuyler! A little help, please!"

"Lucy! Where are you?" Schuyler had landed on the mezzanine over the entrance. The glass-block windows were cracked and tumbling to the floor beside her. She carefully stepped through the rubble to the railing and gasped at the destruction, then she screamed and sprinted.

"Over here! Hurry!" yelled Lucy, hanging by her finger-tips from the balcony railing, twenty feet above the main floor. "My hands are sweaty, and I'm slipping!"

"Lucy!" She reached Lucy just as one hand slipped from the railing. Dropping her sword and shield, Schuyler wrapped both hands around Lucy's arm and tugged her over the balcony wall. Lucy's shield had morphed into the brace-let. "How did this happen? I thought you got tossed down an aisle when the explosion hit."

Sprawled on the floor, Lucy gasped for air, a hand to her breastplate. "I hit the wall, and the shock wave flipped me over the balcony. It seemed like forever before you found me." She managed a weak smile. "Thanks, by the way." A frown settled on her forehead as she looked around. "Where's the daemon? Did you see what happened to him?"

"No clue, girlfriend," said Schuyler with a grimace. She leaned over the railing and pointed. Debris littered the main floor. "At least the Spectrescope isn't hanging with the whale anymore."

"The Spectrescope! Do you see it?" Lucy scrambled to her feet and gasped at the destruction. "How will we ever find it?" Discouragement settled into her bones, her shoulders slumping, her nose throbbing. "I've got to be the worst keeper of the Spectrescope ever. If I were a Norse god, I could call it, and it would come."

"Oh, good idea! Try that," said Schuyler, nodding rapidly. "It is a magical artifact, and it chose you. Why wouldn't that work?" She couldn't keep a big grin from dimpling her cheeks as she saw the lopsided pucker and raised brow on Lucy's face. "Oh c'mon! It's worth a try, girlfriend. Do it!"

"If only to keep you quiet," said Lucy, squinting at her. She leaned over the railing, stuck out a hand, and commanded, "Spectrescope! Come hither!"

Down on the main floor, a pile of broken ceiling tiles and bones began shaking and falling apart. An object zoomed into the air and flew to the girls leaning over the balcony. Schuyler squealed and clapped her hands, bouncing on her feet.

Lucy, openmouthed and dumbfounded, still held her hand in midair as the silver object zipped its way toward her. It slowed, then nestled itself into her hand and glowed, the runes morphing and the ring spinning. Her hand closed over it as she stared at the beloved artifact. Then she dropped and sat on the floor.

"I can't believe that worked," she said, looking up. Schuyler was grinning like a Cheshire cat. "How did I not know this?"

The Spectrescope vibrated in her hand. She waited as a message appeared in the lens. *The stronger your faith, the stronger our bond, and the deeper your access to the High King's power.* "Wow. I love you even more right now. Thank you, Spectrescope." *Love the High King because he first loved you.* Lucy only nodded and smiled.

The Museum of Memories

When Jeannie Hornberger walked through the portal with Helena, the angelic spirit, she knew the next few moments would be painful. The instantaneous transportation from her guest bedroom to the strange place where she stood now had awoken her senses.

The main floor of the museum was lit from above by an ethereal light source. The atmosphere tingled with expectancy, alive and vibrant. It was an odd sensation, and one Jeannie had not experienced in a long time, so long she couldn't remember the last time she felt so energized. Helena stood motionless to the side of the room, watching and waiting as Jeannie explored her surroundings.

The whale bones still hung from the ceiling just as she remembered them, milky white and clean, the amazing design engineered for weight-bearing the massive mammal's form. She gazed lovingly on the superstructure, smiling. "I've missed you, Wally," she whispered. "You were a happy part of my childhood." She remembered the first time she saw the skeleton; she had affectionately called him Wally. Then others started calling him Wally too.

Jeannie wandered among the displays on the main floor, peeking into the glass cabinets at fossils, replicas of dinosaur heads and bones, and vintage clocks and watches. Next came the doll exhibit and the Victorian china dolls with painted faces and frilly lace dresses. The Cabbage Patch Kids were her favorite—always had been—with their puffy, benign doll faces and bodies. She could spend hours at the museum and never tire of it.

Helena stepped close, her hand out and fingers beckoning. "Come, Jeannie. It's time to remember," she said softly. The entity radiated a soft, gentle glow as though she were a ray of diffused sunshine. Jeannie shook her head and took a step back.

"No, I don't want to go. Please don't make me," said Jeannie, ignoring the spirit and faking an interest in a dollhouse display. "I'm fine right here, or we can go back if you want."

"Come, Jeannie," said the spirit, her voice firm. "You must remember and decide. You will receive no more opportunities." Again, she reached her hand toward the woman.

Jeannie trembled and glanced about, then reluctantly took the proffered hand. The spirit led her up the stairs to the balcony and into the mezzanine overlooking the main floor. She gasped. They had just left the pristine room, but the room now was devastated and lay in ruins.

Dust and cobwebs covered the abandoned displays, and the dolls had toppled from their stands, the dresses yellowed and dingy, the houses in disrepair. The floor was dirty, and the beloved Wally the whale hung lopsided, missing several bones and suffering from a broken lower jawbone.

"Oh! What happened here?" asked Jeannie, turning to the spirit.

"You no longer wanted the simple joy that was offered here. You stopped coming," said Helena.

"But that's not true. I only wanted to know more, to see more. What's wrong with that?" said Jeannie defensively.

"Come, there is more to see." Helena turned and beckoned toward a long corridor, flanked on either side by dioramas, each depicting a different moment in Jeannie's timeline. The hall was long and unending, fading away into gloom the farther it went. Here, where they stood, a soft light lit the space but had no source Jeannie could detect. It was warm and comforting, but the gloominess, as the hall went on, chilled her.

Helena stepped to a diorama, her open palm extending an invitation for the woman to view its contents. Jeannie stepped closer and gasped. It was a scene from her childhood. Helena pressed the button next to the window, and the scene activated. It was like watching a three-dimensional movie without the special glasses.

Inside the diorama, younger versions of her mother and father laughed as they gave Christmas gifts to ten-year-old Jeannie and her younger brother. Their golden retriever slept peacefully beside the flickering fireplace, the only warm spot in the old house, his tail whipping back and forth as he dreamed. The large and fragrant spruce Christmas tree twinkled with multicolored lights in the corner, the ornaments reflecting the fire glow.

Happy memories surged through Jeannie's brain as she slumped against the glass, fingers splayed and wishing she could melt through the pane. There it was—the old two-story house with the heating grates in the floor, the drafty windows, and the creaky pipes that moaned when someone turned on the taps. *Oh, those were good times*, she thought. *How I miss you, Poppy. Remember when lightning struck the house, and the surge blew out the bulbs in the antique bathroom sconces?* A tear trickled down her cheek unnoticed. Helena smiled and beckoned again. The scene dimmed; the little family was left frozen in time.

Next came a diorama of a young and boisterous thirteen-going-on-thirty Jeannie with long brown hair, big blue eyes, and a personality as big as Texas. Again, the scene activated, and the teenager tugged Aunt Isabel's hand, leading her through the traveling carnival that had set up in the alley-way between the stores on Division Street. Laughing, they ate cotton candy with sticky purple fingers, and then they played ring toss. Aunt Isabel scored a little stuffed teddy bear that Jeannie promptly claimed as hers. Next, they rode the merry-go-round until the lights blinked, indicating the ride was over, and then they rode again.

Jeannie placed a hand on the glass, another tear slipping down her cheek as the light went out and darkness claimed the memory.

"I don't like this. Please take me back," said Jeannie, a hand clutching the collar of her robe. The entity showed no emotion as she stood next to the dark diorama. Jeannie's head dipped, and her hand fell from the robe. She turned like an automaton and followed the spirit.

Helena crossed the aisle and stood by a much larger diorama, the tall plate glass reaching several feet from side to side. Helena's large, expressive eyes contrasted with the rosy complexion of her skin, and for a fleeting moment, reflected sorrow. Then, without a word, she pressed the button. Jeannie whimpered.

This moment depicted a clear, sunny day. Downtown Grand River Valley was crowded and decorated for the July holiday, flags waving from the lampposts while street vendors sold hotdogs, popcorn, ice-cold lemonades, and sparklers. The last parade float passed by and disappeared as the family waved tiny flags. Jeannie was fourteen, and her brother, Bobby, was eleven. It had been a wonderful day and a sweet memory until a car spun out of control and hit her father as he crossed the street to buy her another coveted hotdog. The brief scene flickered out, and Jeannie slid to the floor, weeping.

A Hunting We Will Go

10

"Let's check the Northern Michigan Habitats. It's the next big room down this corridor," said Lucy, jogging past displays of cougars, foxes, wolves, and coyotes, their formidable faces pointing skyward with silent howls behind the glass panels. The predator exhibits meandered down the winding corridor, the dim lighting showcasing the brilliantly painted backdrops and specimens.

"We still haven't seen the other spirit who took your mom through the portal. What will we do about her?" asked Schuyler, squinting. The light was deceiving. The corridor appeared to be getting longer and changing time periods. It was much older now and dilapidated. "This hall is never ending!"

"We'll figure it out when we find her and my mom."

Finally, they came to a room lined with open wall shelves displaying moles and shrews, chipmunks and squirrels in the small-animal exhibit. Other glass-enclosed scenes occupied the center of the room and lined the walls. The cases were dusty, and cobwebs crowded the corners of the ceiling.

"Ew! That's disgusting," said Schuyler, pointing at the cobwebby shrews and wrinkling her nose. "Poor little guys."

"Shh!" said Lucy, a finger to her lips. "I think our ghost is on the other side of the room near the wetlands habitat," she whispered. Then, staying close to a case that divided the center of the room, she peeked around the side.

Fufurcas was blowing the feathers off the bird specimens from the wetlands display and laughing as the feathers floated about, littering the floor and leaving the little bodies naked. The display's backdrop had melted. The cross section of aquatic life was sinking to the bottom in the softened resin, and he was talking to himself.

"Wait till I get hold of *your* feathers, Helena, then I'll pluck *you* like a chicken!" He laughed, brushed the feathers from his cloak, and strutted toward the exit on the opposite side of the room.

"I don't think so, Fufurcas," said Lucy, stepping out from behind the display, the Spirit Sword pointed at him. "Your reign of terror stops tonight." The spirit swung around, abashed he had not detected their presence, and scowled.

Lucy saw his hand flinch, and she blasted him backward with an energy beam. He crashed into the wetlands display and sank into the softened resin, his booted feet in the air.

Schuyler came around the other side of the display and sent an energy blast at him. He blocked her blow and deflected it toward Lucy.

Lucy raised her shield arm and ducked behind it. It absorbed the blast. Schuyler pulled back, and her beam stopped. It gave the daemon time to roll from the display, his cloak absorbing the gooey resin as he ran at Schuyler.

He pushed a blast of air at her and sent her tumbling backward as he ran toward the small-animal exhibit. Lucy followed him, blasting energy at him. She missed and destroyed a glass enclosure, reducing it to rubble.

Furfurcas swiped another air bomb. It glanced off her shield and blew a display partially from the wall. The tiny pygmy shrew dangled from the fake rock.

Lucy thrust a series of blasts at the daemon. He ducked behind a display, the blows shattering the glass and its contents and knocking tiny specimens from their perches. The daemon yelped, then his hand appeared around the bottom of the pedestal and lobbed a fireball at her. It hit her shield and dissipated.

Schuyler squealed as she rushed into the room, blasting away. But her hurriedly aimed blast hit the wall instead and blew the letters from the small-animal exhibit names, leaving only MO and EW. "Oops," she said, ducking behind a display.

Furfurcas crawled from his hiding place. His staff suddenly appeared in his hand, and he thumped it on the floor. The vibrations rippled through the room, upheaving the remaining displays and toppling them. The plaster walls cracked and shed chunks of drywall, the dust wafting into the air and making it difficult to breathe.

Lucy watched the daemon closely as he smacked the staff in his palm, an open invitation to battle. She stepped within striking distance and stopped. The spirit grinned evilly, his black eyes glittering.

"Oh, so brave, little human. You come at me with your shiny sword, but I have the magician's rod that performed strange and wonderful works in your world. The Prince of the Under Realm, Darnathian, awarded it to me knowingly. You must think I am weak, trying to scare me with your pointy sticks."

"You may have your magic, but I have access to the ancient power. It is not mine but the King's," said Lucy. A nervous sweat dribbled down her back, tickling her and reminding her to be courageous. The sword vibrated in her hand as though to admonish her. Schuyler stood next to her and gave her a glance and a nod.

Furfurcas struck. Lucy's sword shook with the mighty blow. The force pushed her back. Schuyler stepped forward and swung as Lucy fell back, giving Schuyler room to maneuver. The daemon was fast. Moving with the power of several men and holding his staff in the middle, he deflected the strikes. Handgrips had appeared, protecting his hands and wrists, and the ends of the staff had also morphed into sharpened steel, glinting and ominous.

"Together!" yelled Lucy, and together Lucy and Schuyler struck rapidly, their swords a blur. The blades rasped and screeched, steel on steel, a continuous barrage of strikes, but they couldn't get past his staff to strike a vanquishing blow to the daemon.

"Shield down! Ratha-nael, I need you!" shouted Lucy. The sword appeared in her hand as the shield disappeared.

"What're you doing?" yelled Schuyler, fear in her eyes. "You'll be unprotected!"

Without answering, Lucy held both swords, and with a determination she didn't think possible, she struck the staff, shearing off one end of it. The steel blade clanged to the floor and burst into flames. It flared up briefly, smelling of sulfur, and disappeared. Schuyler stood frozen, open-mouthed, and wary.

Furfurcas roared, his anger turning his ruddy face a deeper shade of red, then he turned and fled out the exit, his fur pouf flapping behind him.

An Awakening

11

Helena extended her hand to Jeannie and helped her from the floor. The woman continued to weep, the memory piercing deep into her soul. Finally, she yanked her hand away and turned to leave, but the corridor was gone. Only a mist remained.

"What is this place?" asked Jeannie. Trembling, she waited for the Helena spirit to answer. Instead, the ghost turned aside and pressed another button. The memory diorama activated.

"No, no more! I don't like this," cried Jeannie. "This is just a dream. It must be!"

Inside, her father leaned over his tattered red pickup truck, tinkering with something under the hood. Then he turned and limped to his tool case and retrieved a wrench while teenage Jeannie sat in the cab, sulking and listening to the radio. "We're supposed to be talking, you know, but I'm happy you're spending time with me," said her dad.

A work light suspended from the garage ceiling illuminated his features. The limp she could almost excuse; he'd always had a bad back, but the jagged scar across one cheek was a blaring reminder of her selfishness. He tinkered some more, then peeked around the hood. "I love you, kitten," he said.

"Love you too, Dad," said the teenager, shrugging a shoulder and turning up the radio. The scene blinked out.

"I miss him so much," whispered Jeannie. "Our relationship was never the same after the accident. Mother was always with Dad; he was her focus. I always thought she blamed me for the accident, though she denied it. I blame myself. It's why we always fight when we are together." Her eyes blurred with the memory of a particular argument.

"You are remembering, Jeannie. Your tears will bring release. Now, come and see," said Helena. She walked to another window and pressed the button.

Teenage Jeannie wore her graduation cap and gown, exuberant and glowing, and she was greeting everyone at the party. Banners and balloons floated on the breeze. Food lined a table in the backyard, while another table held gifts and an overflowing box of graduation cards. Her father was grilling burgers on the patio. Her mother placed a plate of veggies on the table, then turned and handed the young graduate a small gift. Beaming widely, her mother waited as Jeannie unwrapped the box and lifted a leather-bound book titled The Chronicles of Ascalon. Disappointment wiped the smile from Jeannie's face as she handed the storybook back to her mother and walked away. The scene faded to nothingness.

Jeannie stayed there, leaning her forehead against the glass, wishing with all her heart she could do everything over and change things.

"You are coming awake, Jeannie," said Helena, glowing softly. "Don't refuse and go back to sleep. The High King loves you; he always has. He has forgiven you and is waiting to be a part of your life." She placed a comforting hand on Jeannie's shoulder as the woman turned to her. "Now, you must forgive yourself."

"Mother and Aunt Isabel have been believers in the spiritual realm for as long as I can remember," said Jeannie. "I knew the High King once, but when Dad had the accident, I decided I didn't believe anymore. Believing only brought more restraints and less freedom. Believing didn't help my dad. The accident shortened his life."

"The High King has given you the ultimate freedom; he offers it freely, releasing you from the past that has kept you in bonds. Your father is free, and he is alive and healthy in Ascalon. The High King is very rich in his kindness and grace." The entity gazed questioningly at her. "Are you awake now, Jeannie?"

Jeannie gazed into the clear blues eyes of the angelic being, and, smiling, she nodded.

Chaos at the Museum

12

"Oh, Jeannie," said Furfurcas, stepping into the corridor. "I don't think you should believe all that nonsense." He laughed as Helena and the woman turned startled expressions to him. "She is such a liar. You can't believe a word she says," he said, pointing at the angelic spirit. "The golden hue is just a ploy."

Jeannie stared wide eyed at the entity in the Santa costume as the stench of sulfur wafted toward her. Her hand clutched her robe closed. She stepped back and bumped into the wall, cowering. The angelic spirit stood in front of her, blocking the daemon.

Helena had transformed in a blink, standing as tall as the angry spirit, the gentle benign expression replaced by fierce determination. She held a glittering broadsword in one hand and a book in the other. Her hair was pulled back by a sparkling band, the tresses cascading over her shoulders and caressing the large white wings on her back. Her stance was regal yet menacing as she spread the wings and raised the sword. Tiny yellow flames licked the edges.

"You shall not take her, Furfurcas," said Helena. She raised the book, the pages falling open. "Let him who thinks he stands take heed that he should not fall."

He casually twirled the restored staff like a baton, the wood rolling over his beefy fingers, and stared at her. "Oh, such is the wisdom of the ages," he sneered. "Do you think you will discourage me with such babble? Or confuse me as you did her?" The staff lay across his fingers. Helena made no response. Slowly, the steel blades reappeared, encompassing each end of the staff as before.

Suddenly, he viciously swung the staff at the angelic spirit. Her sword clashed against the wood, the tiny flames engulfing it as she blocked his strike. The fire flared over the wood, burning it and charring the grain.

"Furfurcas!" Lucy yelled, entering the corridor from a side hallway. She slid to a stop with both swords raised and crossed in front of her. Schuyler entered next, her shield high and sword pointing at the daemon.

The daemon swung his weapon toward them, the blades on either side glinting dangerously. It hissed through the air. Lucy parried the strike, sending his blade sideways with Ratha-nael. He twirled the weapon, the ends circling and deflecting both her swords. Schuyler did a forward thrust, but he deflected her blade too.

Lucy's eyes were watering from the pain of her broken nose; it was difficult to see clearly in the dim corridor. Nevertheless, the angelic being did not enter the conflict. Instead, she flared her wings, protecting Lucy's mom, who was cowering behind the entity.

"Why do you humans trust these spirits?" asked Furfurcas, thumbing at the silent Helena. "They promise peace and prosperity and freedom from your burdens, whatever those are. Do you have peace? Are you rich and prosperous? I think not," he reasoned. "Why not join the Prince of the Under Realm? He has riches beyond measure." His voice was quiet and alluring. He spread his hands in a questioning gesture, his weapon leaned against his leg.

Schuyler's sword dipped as his rhetoric made her sleepy. Lucy prodded her with a foot.

"Schuyler!" said Helena, her voice firm as she raised the book again and read from the pages. "Never tire of kindness or loyalty. These are virtues. Hold to them." Her sword flickered, the tiny flames sparking and spitting.

Schuyler shook her head and raised her sword. "I will," she said, determined not to listen to the daemon anymore. Each time he spoke, she became sleepy and confused.

Lucy had moved a little closer to the daemon while he was expounding the benefits of joining the Under Realm. Gripping the hilts to hold her swords steady, she was ready to strike. The daemon appeared calm, even surrounded by magical artifacts infused with power from the High King. The closer she got to him, the more the stench of sulfur burned her nose and throat. It was overwhelming.

Schuyler sneezed, breaking her concentration. The daemon attacked.

Suddenly, his staff was whirling in his hand as he sliced through the air, missing Schuyler's arm and glancing off her shield. Lucy added her swords to the melee and struck with one sword, then the other. Metal screeched against metal, clanking and rasping. Lucy stepped forward, attacked, and retreated as Schuyler took her turn at the daemon.

Their arms were getting tired, and the battle raged on.

The daemon lunged, his arms thrust forward. He barreled into Lucy and crushed her against the wall. Lucy managed to shove him away. Schuyler lunged then, her weight-bearing foot forward. She knocked the weapon from his hands.

The daemon growled and reached for Schuyler, but she kicked him in the chest. He stumbled backward. Lucy charged with both swords and ran him through.

But he didn't implode.

Schuyler's mouth fell open, then closed with a pop as she thrust her sword into the daemon. He wavered on his feet, his face angry and red, glaring at the three gaping wounds. He couldn't move. The power of the swords had rendered him powerless.

"Puny humans," he growled. "You cannot destroy me."

"This is true," said Lucy, dropping the Ratha-nael sword into the sheath.

A blue gemstone in the Belt of Truth wiggled loose and popped into her hand. "I can do nothing without the High King's consent," she said. She swallowed and read the message within the stone. "*As smoke is blown away by the wind, may you blow away too.*" She broke the stone against the tiles, releasing a blue vapor. It swirled around the daemon, who cursed and thrashed, but the smoke wrapped him in coils, binding him.

A scream shattered the air, but it wasn't the daemon. Jeannie swayed, her eyes rolling back, and fainted to the floor with a thump.

Another stone popped from the belt. Lucy quietly read the message before she broke the stone. "*As the wax melts before the fire, so the wicked will perish from before the High King.*" When the vapor evaporated, blue wax covered the daemon like a giant Santa-shaped candle. Lucy and Schuyler just stared, dumbfounded.

Without speaking, Helena stepped forward and touched the flaming sword to the daemon.

He blazed for a moment, then melted in a fiery puddle, the flames consuming the wax. The remains wafted tendrils of smoke into the air. Helena leaned forward and blew away the smoke. The daemon was vanquished.

"Wowza," said Lucy and Schuyler in unison.

Lucy stared at the beautiful Helena, who had returned to her more diminutive, sophisticated form. The sword, the book, and the wings were gone. Though the angelic being looked benign, she was still an incredible spirit, and she made Lucy more than a little nervous.

Helena kneeled next to Lucy's mom on the floor and gently smoothed the hair from Jeannie's face. "She has been through much, but her future is bright now. So you need not worry, Gatekeeper." Helena lifted Jeannie from the floor as though she were a child, then turned to leave. A portal had opened behind her with its spinning light circle.

"Where are you taking her?" asked Lucy, stepping toward them. She didn't know what she could do against this spirit, but she wasn't letting it take her mom.

"I am taking her home. The McGoos are waiting," said Helena, nodding toward the portal.

Through the circle, Lucy could see her benefactors waiting inside the guest bedroom. Mr. Bill grinned and waved frantically, and Ms. Vivian clapped and giggled like a schoolgirl.

"Don't forget your swords," said Helena, then she stepped through the portal. Lucy and Schuyler scrambled for their swords, which had been left unchanged after the daemon was vanquished. Finally, they jumped together through the circle and were greeted enthusiastically by the McGoos.

"Well, that was quite an exciting night at the museum," said Schuyler, nodding thoughtfully, a hand to her chin.

Lucy busted out laughing.

Epilogue

Ms. Vivian was up early on Saturday to bake her famous chocolate chip cookies and a batch of her double-chocolate oatmeal cookie bars. Mr. Bill was busy tucking presents under the restored Christmas tree. Jeannie hummed as she set the plates and cutlery on the dining room table, and her mother, Leona, cut and prepared the vegetables for grilling while chatting with Ms. Vivian.

Dale had blown the surprise earlier in the week when he asked if Rebecca Williams was bringing her triple-berry chocolate torte to the party. Oops.

Upstairs, Lucy yawned and stretched as she lay in bed watching the snow drift past the window; they would have a white Christmas this year, and the school term was out for the holiday break. Her best friend, Schuyler, snored on the inflatable mattress beside the bed.

Delicious aromas wafting from the kitchen made her mouth water and her stomach grumble. She leaned over the edge of the bed and pulled a lock of Schuyler's curls.

"Ouch! What the hay, girlfriend?" asked Schuyler as she sat up and yawned. "Ooh, wait, something smells yummy!"

"Knew it!" Lucy did a fist pump. "Food. It works every time!" She did a happy wiggle on the bed. Though she would have preferred to jump on the bed, you couldn't jump on a memory foam mattress. Schuyler swatted her with the pillow.

"C'mon, we need to claim the bathroom before Dale does. He takes forever." Lucy lunged from the bed, grabbed clothes from the closet, and disappeared down the hall. Schuyler got her overnight pack and stumbled toward the bathroom, yawning.

After brunch, the festivities began. First, there were board games in the dining room, and after they pushed the furniture back to make space, they played ring toss in the living room while Grandma Elliot curled up on the couch with a blanket and a leather-bound book. She smiled as she watched the others competing at the games. Then Rebecca and Stephen Williams, Schuyler's parents, joined the group, bringing more food to the menu. Mr. Williams brought his monster burgers to grill, and Rebecca brought the famous torte. Finally, Lucy and Schuyler built a snowman in the front yard and traced goofy faces in the snow on the hoods of the cars in the driveway.

The day went quickly, and everyone was stuffed and pleasantly tired by the evening. The women gathered around the dining table, exchanging recipes and the latest news, and Dale and Mr. Williams played video games in the small den. Lucy and Schuyler took mugs of hot chocolate to the living room and settled on the floor next to the Christmas tree. Mr. Bill had his feet propped up on the ottoman, reading the newspaper.

"Mr. Bill?" said Lucy. "May I ask you a question?" She set her hot chocolate on a tray, careful not to spill on the light-colored carpet. The glow from the Christmas lights was comforting. It felt natural somehow that they should all be together in this home for Christmas.

"Hmm?" said Bill, lowering the paper and looking at her over the top of his glasses. "What question was that?"

"When I was fighting the daemon, I asked the Spectrescope to seal the room, but it didn't keep him from getting away. It seemed something had weakened the seal. Why is that?" Schuyler put her chocolate down and listened.

"Well, you went off on your own, didn't you? You were relying on your abilities and not on the High King. It seems you thought *you* could do it in your power, isn't that right?" Mr. Bill smiled kindly at her, but his words were clear.

"Yeah," Lucy admitted. "I got a little ahead of things, didn't I?" A dimple appeared in her puckered cheek.

"Self-reliance is a good thing sometimes, but when you rely more on your abilities and not on the High King, it weakens the power you have available to you."

"The Spectrescope said, '*The stronger your faith, the stronger our bond, and the deeper your access to the High King's power.*' I think I understand now." She got up and hugged him. "I love you, Mr. Bill."

"And just so you know, I love you too, Lucy girl," he said with a wink. Then, laying the paper aside and wiggling his toes in his socks, he got up and stretched.

"Mr. Bill—what were you and Ms. Vivian doing while we were fighting it out with the daemon at the museum?"

"Why, we were guarding the portal. You didn't need any more spirits showing up, now did you?" He waggled his eyebrows, then padded to the kitchen. "Hey, Viv," he shouted. "We got any of those double-chocolate cookie bars left?"

Lucy snorted. "He's almost as bad as you are with food," she said, smirking at Schuyler.

"Oh, you're so funny," said Schuyler, handing her a gift. "Here, unwrap this."

"Are we exchanging gifts tonight?" asked Lucy, pulling the paper off and opening the box. "*Schuyler!*" shouted Lucy, chagrined and holding up an ornament.

Dangling from the ribbon was a small red pickup truck with a Christmas tree and brightly colored presents in the back. In the driver's window was painted a little white ghost.

Schuyler scrunched her nose and snickered.

A Note from the Author

Woo-hoo! Thank you for taking this quick, fun adventure with me through the museum. It has always been a place of fun, learning, and imagination. Visit your local museum often and see what sparks your imagination.

I hope after reading Lucy and Jeannie's adventure, you will understand and come awake like Jeannie. The past is the past; we can't change it, but we can move forward and be the best we can be with the High King's help when we find forgiveness, understanding, and love.

Be sure to join Lucy and Schuyler as The Issachar Gatekeeper adventures continue in *The Ghost You Can't See*. You can find more information at www.lgnixon.com.

Blessings!

Scripture References

- Psalm 34:16: "The face of the LORD is against those who do evil, to blot out their name from the earth."

- Psalm 55:22: "Cast your cares on the LORD and he will sustain you; he will never let the righteous be shaken."

- Psalm 68:2: "May you blow them away like smoke—as wax melts before fire, may the wicked perish before God."

- Matthew 6:25: "Therefore I tell you, do not worry about your life, what you will eat or drink; or about your body, what you will wear. Is not life more than food, and the body more than clothes?"

- Ephesians 1:7: "He is so rich in kindness and grace that he purchased our freedom with the blood of his Son and forgave our sins" (NLT).
- 1 Corinthians 10:12 "Therefore let him who thinks he stands take heed that he does not fall" (NASB).

L. G. Nixon grew up hoping to one day become a writer, and after a long career in office management, she began writing. She also grew up in a creaky old house where relatives told of ghostly visitations. Her joy as a writer comes from being able to share the stories God lays on her heart. She creates her otherworldly realms in Michigan, where she lives with her husband, a high-energy boxer dog named Cali, and a tailless cat named Pan. She enjoys motorcycling and skiing, landscape painting, and hopes someday to finish her pilot's license. (She wants to fly the Space Shuttle, if they relaunch it, which means she might need that pilot's license!)

If you are enjoying The Issachar Gatekeeper series, drop her a note. She would love to hear from you!

Visit her website at: www.lgnixon.com